THE AUSTRALIA STORIES

a novel by

Todd James Pierce

MacAdam/Cage Publishing
155 Sansome Street, Suite 550
San Francisco, CA 94104
www.macadamcage.com
Copyright © 2003 by Todd James Pierce
ALL RIGHTS RESERVED

Library of Congress Cataloging-in-Publication Data

Pierce, Todd James, 1965—
The Australia stories a novel / by Todd James Pierce.
p. cm.
ISBN 1-931561-28-1(Hardcover : alk. paper)
1. Blue Mountains (N.S.W. : Mountains)—Fiction.
2. Missing persons—Fiction. 3. Grandmothers—Fiction.
4. Mothers—Fiction. 5. Australia—Fiction. 6. Hiking—Fiction.
I. Title.
PS3616.I36 A96 2003
813'.6—dc21

                                        2002153639

Portions of this novel have appeared elsewhere, in slightly different
form: "Smoke" in *American Literary Review*, "The Australia Stories"
in *The Literary Review*, "Love" in *The Missouri Review*, and
"Coachman's Paddock" in *The Seattle Review*.

Manufactured in the United States of America
10 9 8 7 6 5 4 3 2 1

Book design by Dorothy Carico Smith.

Publisher's Note: This is a work of fiction. Names, characters,
places, and incidents either are the product of the author's
imagination or are used fictitiously. Any resemblance to actual
events, locales, or persons, living or dead, is entirely coincidental.

THE AUSTRALIA STORIES

a novel by
Todd James Pierce

MacAdam/Cage

COACHMAN'S PADDOCK
1979

The year I lived in Australia, my best friend was Tommy Jameson. Tommy was a tall, long-limbed boy, who had lived in the mountains all his life. He often wore an Australian rabbit-pelt hat called an Akurba and on cold days an oilskin riding coat that fell in a long, straight line below his knees. He read a great deal and knew things about the world I did not, though we were the same age, thirteen, and attended classes together. When we met he asked if I was from Los Angeles the city or Los Angeles the state. I thought it a ridiculous question, that is, until he took me to the world map displayed in our history class and pointed first to a city marked "LA" and then to the state of Louisiana, which bore the same initials. "The city," I said. "I'm from Los Angeles the city."

"And this other Los Angeles," he asked, "it's not the state, is it?"

"No, it's Louisiana."

"Well, fair enough," he laughed, then put his hands in his pockets as if he didn't know what to say next.

Some afternoons we would walk down to Sweet Gully Falls, and on others to Silverton Valley. My favorite place, however, was Coachman's Paddock, a long field where wallabies sunned themselves. We sat in a blue gum on a platform he'd built some years before. Below us, wallabies entered the paddock, first the males then females and joeys. They'd stay there until evening, basking and playboxing. They'd eat grass and use their forepaws to smoothe back their fur.

Over time, I learned their names, Redwhig, Doona, and Flathead being Tommy's favorites. Redwhig was the oldest male. If we moved too close, he would make a loud clicking sound, urging the others toward the protection of trees. The mob would tuck in their forepaws and raise their tails before pulling into the air, propelled by their thick back legs. But most days, we simply stayed in our tree, sunlight webbing through spear-shaped leaves, while we ate Tim Tam bars and cornish pasties left over from lunch. Sometimes he would ask about my life in America: what was it like to have thirteen TV channels, was it true some stores were open twenty-four hours a day, and how come everyone ate so many hamburgers? Some questions, however, I didn't know the answers to, like why did America make Australia sell plutonium, and how come "you Yanks were so keen on us Aussies jumping into the Vietnam War?" I said we must have needed plutonium real bad and, as for Vietnam, I admitted I didn't know, but said my father had gone there as well, which seemed to satisfy him.

As for me, I asked about the wallabies. He told me Redwhig had fathered most of the joeys and that in a few weeks he would challenge the other males again. Doona, a female, could be identified by the white streak edging down her nose, and her joey, a young male named Flathead, had dark brown ears that were usually pushed back. I came to like Flathead the most, the way he tentatively moved around the adults, curiosity evident in his features. I noticed how he playboxed with the other males, butting his head and rocking back on his tail, his mother never far from him; but one day in mid-October he moved into the mob and stayed there. We kept waiting for him to return, but he never did.

That night Tommy and I walked home, fascinated by what we'd seen. Above us, trees opened to a leaden sky. We heard the chatter of cockatoos—or cockies, as Tommy called them—and beyond that, a breeze moving over distant hills. When we entered town, Tommy asked, "What animals did you used to see in the States?"

"Sometimes coyotes would dig through our trash, but I never saw them."

"Coyotes are kind of like dogs," he asked, "aren't they?"

"Like wild dogs."

"We don't have any wild dogs around here," he said, "but up north they have dingoes. Abos use them for hunting."

He grew quiet, and I sensed something from him I had not sensed before, a frustration that seemed out of character. As we walked back, he kept his head down, his hands deep in his pockets. We stopped at my uncle's nursery, and for a moment I felt I didn't know him, though in many ways we were alike. We both lived in the mountains with single mothers, we both went to the same school, we both felt awkward at times around people older than us. "Ta," he said, which was an Australian way of saying goodbye. Then he continued down the road that sloped to the edge of town.

My uncle's nursery was a small corner lot, seedlings toward the front, roses and fruit trees in the back. On this afternoon, my mother was sitting at a sandstone table, sipping tea, while my uncle watered seedlings. Behind them, two elderly customers looked at hanging ferns, examining the small white price tags attached to each pot.

"So where were you today?" my mother asked.

"Out at Coachman's Paddock," I said.

"Out at the paddock?" she mused. "Shouldn't you be home studying?"

"I'll study tonight," I said.

My uncle walked over to us, wearing his usual work clothes, a white dress shirt and khaki pants. With his right hand, he crimped the garden hose in two, restricting its flow. "Oh, give the poor lad a break," he said. "When I was his age, I was making secret excursions into the city, as you well know."

"When *you* were his age," my mother said, "you were at the top of your class."

"And heaps of good it does me," he said, half-joking.

"It got you exactly what you wanted," she said, "and you know it."

"I know nothing of the kind." He knelt to turn off the spigot. "So tell me, Sparrow, what's troubling you in school?"

"History," I said. "History's the worst of it."

"All that George Washington stuff's not big over here, is it?"

"Not really. I have trouble with the lords and kings and governors."

"The kings and governors," he said. "I'm very good with them, especially the cute ones."

"Oh, knock it off, Bill," my mother said. "Now's not the time."

"You have to remember this," he explained. "From a certain perspective, Oz and the States are a lot alike. If you go back far enough, we have the same history, a bunch of weasely old buggers sitting around Westminster Abbey with nothing better to do than hire ships. So it's only the last two hundred years you really have to worry about." He folded his hands into his lap. "As for royalty, you have to remember three things. Elizabeth is queen now. George the Second was the crazy one. And Victoria was the mean old broad who needed to lay off the bickies and jam."

"Bill," my mother scolded, "you may think you're helping, but you're not."

"Now, Sam," he continued, "who was the loony king?"

"George the Second," I replied.

"And who's queen now?"

"Elizabeth," I answered.

"And the one who needed to get in line for a slimming course?"

"Victoria."

My mother merely shook her head.

"See," my uncle said, "he knows as much about history as any boy in these hills and will do just fine during his year abroad."

My mother was absently gazing at potted azaleas arranged in the distance. Then she turned to us. "I would like him to learn some of the things I know. I understand it's a hard request, but one I think important."

"He will," my uncle said, "but in his own time."

That night I left the nursery feeling better. I thought my life held some greater purpose and that my personality would soon expand, though I wasn't sure how that would happen. My uncle's advice, however, was not particularly helpful because we were no longer studying royalty, but the great westward expansion, how Australians set up dairy farms and sheep stations across the outback. At home, my mother fixed us grilled cheese sandwiches, which we ate while watching TV. After dinner, I riddled my way through our history book. A man named Edward Hargraves, I read, started a gold rush in New South Wales. But two weeks later I had trouble remembering his name for our exam. I sat there, looking at our history teacher, who we called Old Patterson, noticing the cool distance in his eyes.

Afterward, Tommy told me, "Old Patterson's a bloke who lives in the past."

"I don't think I did so well," I said.

"We weren't supposed to. He just wants us to know how dumb we are."

"But that doesn't seem fair," I protested.

"My mum says the same thing."

In the weeks that followed I saw a new mood settle over Tommy: he let his hair grow, he began to wear his T-shirts untucked, and once he came to school with scratches on his arms and legs. At lunchtime, he no longer played rugby. In history, he wasn't engaged by Old Patterson's quizzes. Instead he looked out the windows, his eyes focused on something far away.

For the most part, I spent my afternoons with my uncle. He was teaching me about the nursery so I might help him during the busy months of November and December, though some days Tommy and I still ventured to the Paddock. The wallabies now ate long stems of grass and lay in the shade, a new tenseness worked between them. The males stretched to show their height; the females remained in groups. On one of these days, while we sat in a tree watching Redwhig, Tommy asked, "Back in the States, you ever date a girl?"

"I went with Susan Lewis to my sixth-grade dance, but it wasn't a real date."

"Did you like her?"

"Kind of," I said. I moved to a slightly higher branch and let my legs hang over the limb. "You ever go on a date?"

"Naw," he said. "Most blokes around here don't date until Year Eight or Nine. It's not respectful to go seeing girls much earlier than that."

"If I was back home, I'd go on dates. I'd get my dad to drive."

"I wouldn't want my dad to drive me anywhere on a date. That'd be bloody awful. It'd mess up everything."

"Mess up everything about what?" I said.

"Ah, you don't know nothing about nothing," he said, then turned from me.

By now the sky was filled with evening colors: clouds touched with raspberry, coal shadows sheeted against peaks. Below us, Redwhig approached Doona, but Doona hopped away. Cautiously Tommy asked, "What do you think of Jeannie O'Dell?"

"She's kind of nice," I said. "She's pretty."

"I think so, too," he said, but then he corrected himself. "I mean, I don't mind being around her that much."

"I kind of like some of the girls at school."

"You ever kissed a girl?"

"Not really," I said. "Have you?"

"Naw, but my brothers told me about it some. They said to make your lips real soft. And to put your arms around the girl real tight."

He sat next to me, folding then unfolding his hands. Finally he put his arm across my shoulders, his way of apologizing for what he'd said earlier. We were quite close then, two boys on the edge of manhood. I liked sitting next to him, but understood we might not always be close. There was a sadness at his house, a sadness I wasn't old enough to fully understand, but sensed was important. The sun pulled itself behind the mountains, the sky absorbing its champagne ghost. "So who do you like?" he asked.

His words had a sudden baring effect on me. He had probably seen me look at Kelly Richardson, a girl who, like us, was in Year Seven.

"Come on," he said. "I know you like somebody."

"Kelly," I finally said, and as I said this I felt for the first time something like desire open inside me. "I kind of like Kelly Richardson," I confessed.

"I thought so," he said, then made a curious clicking sound.

We stayed there longer than usual. Below us, Redwhig urged the mob toward trees where they would find their secret places of sleep. That night, we returned long after seven, my uncle's nursery already closed. At home, my mother asked, "The Paddock?"

"The Paddock," I admitted.

"Let's not make a habit of it, OK?"

"OK," I said, but saw how she looked at me, her eyes holding a question. We ate dinner in front of the TV, and later I went to my room, where I studied history. By now our class had moved on to World War I, in which Australian Diggers were commissioned alongside English troops. That night I had even more difficulty than usual concentrating, but I was starting to understand how everything fit together: America, Australia, even England itself.

At school, two days later, Tommy arrived with Jeannie O'Dell. I saw how they looked at each other, their gaze holding a strange hope, but no one else appeared to notice. They had done nothing more than walk to school—he had not carried her books, they had not held hands—but still there was something about their presence that made me believe they were feeling the first pinpricks of love. We were only in Year Seven. Love was supposed to be beyond our world, but even then, I knew Tommy could not wait for time to pass. His heart was ruled by an emptiness he could not fill. When they reached the netball courts, they parted, their arms touching as though by accident.

Throughout the morning, I saw how Tommy was interested in his studies again, taking good notes and answering questions in both English and math. I noticed, too, that he fidgeted, and when he spoke, his words ran together. At lunch I hoped to talk with him, but he spent it with Jeannie and her friends. So instead I joined a game of rugby. Occasionally I would look at them relaxing by the sidelines. Kelly Richardson sat with them as well. And now, seeing her, I realized I did in fact like her a great deal. Each time she looked my way, I felt clumsy and my thoughts fogged over. Near the end of the game, when I dropped an easy lateral, another boy walked over to me and said, "Don't they have chooks in the States?"

"Chooks?" I asked.

"You know, girls—don't they have girls?"

"Plenty," I said.

"Then you should know how to forget about them and concentrate on the game."

"I do," I said.

But the fact was, I didn't. I enjoyed looking at her, how she sat on the freshly cut grass, looking back at us. Like other girls, she was dressed in her school uniform: a white blouse and a green tartan skirt. She sat with her legs folded under her, talking with Jeannie and Tommy, who was doing his best to appear disinterested. When the bell sounded, my teammates and I were in a scrum, our arms joined, all of us trying to move the ball with our feet, but then the energy of the game left us. We were students once again. I collected my books and saw Tommy waiting for me.

"You could've invited me over," I said.

"You could've invited yourself. We were only sitting there."

"You were only sitting there because Jeannie O'Dell likes you," I said.

He did not respond to this accusation, but considered it, looking off at the hills. "Tomorrow afternoon," he began, "Jeannie and I are going to skip sixth period and walk behind the school."

"If you're asking me to cover for you, I will."

"That's not it," he said. "I think Kelly might go if you ask."

"What do you mean?"

"Tomorrow," he said. "I think she likes you."

"She told you that?"

"No," he said, "she told Jeannie and Jeannie told me."

Right then, the second bell rang and the schoolyard emptied except for us. We stood by the rugby field, our books at our feet, jackets folded over our arms.

For the rest of the day, I could think of nothing other than Kelly Richardson: her hair pulled back into a ponytail, her thin blonde eyebrows so light they were nearly invisible, her almost-pink lips. I was holding a warm, expansive secret, an emotion that could fill me if I let it. I couldn't name these feelings, but knew they were something like love, like the feelings my father felt for my mother, back when they first met, though I also knew these same feelings were not enough to keep them together.

After school, I went to my uncle's nursery. As soon as

I got there I started on my chores. By the time I'd finished sweeping, my uncle had taken a seat near the wooden shack where he kept the till, two cups of tea on the sandstone table before him. I stirred a spoonful of sugar into mine. I liked working in his nursery because it was outside the regular world, a sanctuary where new plants arrived each day, where people bought seedlings and sacks of rose food, and where the general chaos of life was kept at bay. "Well, Sparrow," he said, "how's history?"

"History's OK," I said. "We're up to World War II."

"World War II," he mused. "Good stuff there. You'll like that."

"Why?" I asked.

"I'm not going to give it away. You can't have all of your lessons taught here. I mean, it's not right for me to put some poor schoolmaster out of a job, now is it?"

"Just tell me, Uncle Bill."

"Loose lips sink ships," he said. "I'll tell you only this. It's about your country and my country. And already I've given away too much. I can't say any more, so don't ask."

"Uncle Bill," I whined. "Come on, tell me."

"Nope," he said, then in a gesture of pantomime, he

zipped his lips shut.

"If you don't tell me, I might get distracted and overwater the seedlings."

"You would not."

"I might," I said.

He raised one eyebrow, then looked at me cockeyed. "Since you put it that way, I'll give you the general idea, but don't go blaming me when some poor schoolmaster ends up on the dole." He set his tea on the table. "Your country saved our country at the end of World War II. If it wasn't for America, we'd be flying the Japanese flag right now."

"Nah-ah," I said.

"We would, too," he replied. "We'd be flying the Japanese flag, doing the Tokyo Tango, and eating lots of rice." Then he put his arm around me. "You know what, Sparrow? You should've been born fifty years ago. Americans were very popular here in the fifties. You'd have been flavor of the month, all year long." Then he must have seen something in me, some small nervousness or distraction. "But you're not thinking about history today, are you?"

"Not really," I said.

He leaned toward me, lowering his voice, making me feel as though the town had shrunk so that we were its only two occupants. "I know your mother's hard on you, but it's because she wants you to do well here."

"She's not *that* hard," I said.

"You know, our father was a very strict man."

"I know," I said.

"We used to sneak out when we were kids. Your mum ever tell you that?"

"No," I said.

"On Saturdays, we'd go to the city. We'd see movies. We'd take the ferry around the Harbour." He shifted in his seat, lifting his cup, then setting it down. "What I mean is, you're getting to the age where you need to be your own person. Life has a fair amount of goodness in it, but most people don't know how to find it. I'm a small man. I own a house and lease a corner nursery, but it's all I've ever wanted. It satisfies me. You should find things that satisfy you as well, don't you agree?"

"I guess so," I said, but as I said this, my eyes began to focus on things behind him. On seedlings, then jasmine, then finally on a girl just outside his nursery. Kelly Richardson. She stood beside the roadside placard, her green jumper tied around her waist. She looked at me with such purpose I knew she would say yes, that she might be reluctant, but eventually she would agree to walk with me the following day.

History seemed to take forever. Old Patterson lectured about Australia's involvement in World War II: shortly after Pearl Harbor, bombs were dropped on the northern city of Darwin and a Japanese sub was hoisted from Sydney Harbour. But as he talked, I felt he was staring at us—Tommy, Jeannie, Kelly and me. He paid special attention to Tommy, who didn't take notes but instead looked at Jeannie, then at the window, then at Jeannie again.

When we finally left, I had a sour feeling in my stomach and couldn't believe no one tried to stop us. I was glad when we reached the opening in the fence. Tommy went first, followed by Jeannie, then Kelly and me.

We walked a little ways down Cooper's Trail, past gravillea bushes and tree stumps, the valley opening as far as we could see: withered limbs of gum trees, cliffs rising like burnished steel, ferns draped over sandstone peaks. The sun was straight above, erasing almost every shadow. By the time we were past the school parking lot, Tommy had sidled up beside Jeannie and taken her hand, a firm, direct gesture she did not question or refuse. I wanted to hold Kelly's hand, but when I moved close I felt something between us, a thickness that was not between Tommy and his girl, but then she let her arm fall against mine.

We were only a little ways from school, not even a quarter mile, but already in a world where the earth was red, where cockatoos speckled far-off trees and the sounds of the city disappeared entirely. Tommy and Jeannie wandered off toward a line of trees, not far from us, where ashen trunks corkscrewed into the air supporting only a thin canopy of leaves. Kelly and I sat on a large rock and looked at the pocked valley below.

"Where are they going?" I asked.

"Oh, them," she said, "they're off to pash."

"Pash?" I asked.

"You know, pash, passion, snog, make out."

"Oh," I said.

She turned toward me, her blue eyes fixed in a way that dared me not to look away. "You know what I like best about you? The way you speak. You speak like people on TV."

"I don't speak much different than you."

"Heaps different. You do your vowels wrong. Like when you say *history*, you don't say it right, or when you say something like *kookaburra*."

"Well, teach me how to say it," I said.

"That's just it," she said. "You make all the vowels long. It's very American. Try making them short." Then she demonstrated: "K*ook-a*-b*u*rr-*a*."

"Kookaburra," I said, imitating her.

She laughed then. "That's not it at all. K*ook-a*-b*u*rr-*a*. Kookaburra."

"Kookaburra," I said, which made her laugh again.

"Ah, mate, you're hopeless. You're as Yank as they come."

"Kookaburra," I said.

"Now stop it. You're only making fun of me."

"Kookaburra," I said.

"I don't think you'll ever get it. People from the States just don't understand."

I took her hand, which made her stop laughing. She studied me with that same direct gaze, those eyes that

I felt could see more in me than I could see in myself. I put my hand on her hip. "Do you pash?" I asked.

"I don't pash," she said. "But I will kiss you."

I moved toward her, and remembering what Tommy had told me, I made my lips as soft as I could. I touched them against hers for a quick, sweet moment, one where we were no longer two entirely separate people. After we parted, I looked at her, the delicate lines of her face, the way her lips remained open, just a little. I tried to hold on to this sensation, but already knew I wouldn't be able to hold it for as long as I wanted.

"That was nice," she said, folding her hand around mine and drawing it to her.

I was about to say the same, but heard footsteps behind us, leather-soled shoes moving up the hill. There, on the trail, I saw Old Patterson. His face seemed more wrinkled in direct sun. He still wore his blue coat, though sweat dampened his chest. He gave us a look of pure disappointment. He surveyed the area, clearly confused, but then his attention settled on the trees where Tommy had taken Jeannie. "I thought there were four of you," he said, then cupped his hands around his mouth. "Mr. Jameson," he called, "I would like to see you. I would like to see you, Mr. Jameson." He cocked his head, listening. "Mr. Jameson," he yelled. "Don't make me go over there and find you."

The air was amazingly still: no cockatoos, no magpies, not even a throaty old kookaburra offering its laugh. There was only the sound of a distant breeze. "I don't know," Old Patterson began, "what brings young people to a place like this. I mean, how can young people be so careless with their lives? Actions have consequences," he said, "and consequences do not always go away." He clasped his hands the way he did during lecture. "Do you understand what I'm saying?" he asked.

I had no idea what he was saying, but before we could answer, Tommy and Jeannie emerged, the sun brilliant upon them: he no longer wore his tie, and the top two buttons of her blouse remained undone. I was surprised to see them like this, though in another way, I understood. As they approached, I saw anger worked across his face, a defiance I'd never felt. My own face, I knew, revealed fear and respect, but I wanted it to show courage, mainly for Kelly's sake. She sat at my side, her feet crossed at the ankle, her fingers tucked under her thighs, waiting patiently for whatever punishment might come our way.

"I would like to know, Mr. Jameson, what you think you were doing down there?"

"We weren't doing nothing," Tommy said, looking away from Old Patterson.

"If you weren't doing anything, why did you need to come here? We have plenty of places on campus where you can do nothing."

At this, Tommy stiffened.

"The school will call all of your parents. I don't want to disappoint them, but I see no way around it."

"My folks are often disappointed," Jeannie said.

Old Patterson turned hard eyes upon her. "How old are you, Jeannie?" he snapped.

Instead of answering, she crossed her arms.

"How old?" he summoned.

"Thirteen," she said.

"Yes, thirteen," Old Patterson said. "And at thirteen, do you think you understand your world?"

She simply stared at him.

"Do you understand what your life is about? Or

what your life will be like ten years from now?"

"Oh, lay off," Tommy said. His voice wavered, revealing more than he'd wanted.

Old Patterson looked at the sky, his eyes thin. I thought he'd lecture us again, but instead he removed his wallet and selected a photo of a girl who appeared to be our age. She sat in a Queen Anne chair, her dark hair clipped straight at her shoulders. "Miss O'Dell, how old would you say this girl here is?"

"Oh, bugger off," Tommy said.

"Yes, this girl, Jeannie, take a look," he said, directing the photo at her. "She's fifteen. Two years older than you. But unlike you, she has an eight-month-old daughter. Eight months," he mused. "You're good at math, Jeannie. You can figure out how old she was when this happened."

But Jeannie only offered a smug smile meant to hide her true feelings.

"She doesn't go to school anymore," Old Patterson continued. "She spends her days at home, with her own mother. They'll be no Certificate for her, no university, no Tafe, no job training." His gaze swept over Kelly and me, then he turned back to Tommy. "The child's father works in a mine, twelve hours a day. Do you understand what I am saying, Mr. Jameson? He works for United Opal, out near Dubbo, and even there he makes half of what your mother makes."

Tommy did not answer. Instead, he sighed as if he were bored, though I could tell he was not bored, only scared, as I was.

"I do not want any of you to waste your lives in this manner. History can teach you things if you let it."

He waited for his words to sink in, and when they did, he buttoned his jacket, then addressed me: "And as for you, Mr. Browne, I'd like you to remember that you're a guest in our country. You'll be with us only a year, if I'm not mistaken?"

I nodded, but apparently that was not enough for him. "Yes," I said.

"OK then," Old Patterson concluded. "Please keep that in mind."

We began to walk up that narrow trail, toward Johnson's Point, then over to the school. Tommy and Jeannie walked before us, their feet shuffling through the dust. They did not look at anything—the mountains, the valley, even the school—but kept their eyes turned down, studying the worn path. In that moment, I saw my life so clearly. I was a small, hopeful boy who would do the best he could under the rules of this world. Tommy, however, was not like that at all. His heart had been broken and put back together in such a way all the pieces did not fit as well as he wanted them to. Once on school grounds, I looked to Kelly and tried to offer an apology with my eyes. Then she did the nicest thing a girl had ever done for me: she hooked her pinkie around mine, held it for a moment, then released it.

That day, I took my time walking home. I felt older, as though my presence filled more of the world than it had just that morning. I walked all the way to Cathedral Heights before cutting down to Coachman's Paddock, where the wallabies seemed to be waiting for my arrival. Their eyes were turned toward me, but as I approached I saw they were not actually looking at me but at Redwhig and another male named Gulliver. They were fighting for the benefit of Doona, who stood watching them kick and bite and finally fall into thick brown weeds that covered the earth. I understood I was watching a rare sight, but on that day I didn't care. I was still thinking about Kelly and what Old Patterson had said to me.

When I arrived home I found my mother on the front veranda. I walked up slowly, past flowers my uncle had planted, until I stood at the base of the steps. "I know you're mad," I said, but she didn't yell at me. She simply moved a manuscript page into her discard pile, then looked at me.

"I'm not mad at you for seeing a girl," she said. "But you shouldn't sneak off during school hours."

"I know," I said.

She moved toward me, a sadness evident in her eyes and in the way she held her arms close to her body, and I wondered if she'd been thinking about my father. It was strange to think about him because his life was more or less the same as when I'd lived with him—he still worked at the bank; he still watched the news with dinner—but my life had changed so much since I'd moved to Australia. My mother met me at the top step, her arms crossed between us, then she combed her fingers through my hair. We did not move for a moment, the space between us different and unfamiliar. "You know," she finally said, "I was young once, too." She patted my back in a way that made me feel very good about myself, as though I were just the person I was supposed to be, though I did not often feel like that.

That night, while eating dinner, I noticed something about my mother I had not noticed before: she was a pretty woman with delicate features and long, slender hands my father must have admired. She was the type of woman who would hold on to her beauty for many years, but I didn't think she would remarry. Already she'd found a type of solace in divorce, working each day, reading most nights.

Outside, as we sat in our wicker chairs and drank tea, a lightness moved between us, the type of comfort and goodwill I associated with my earliest childhood memories, a natural ease I have since lost. "You know," she began, "your Uncle Bill thinks this is all his fault."

"All what?" I asked.

"How you went off today. He says he told you something about 'being your own man.'"

"It's not his fault," I said. "I did it on my own."

"You should tell him that. Sometimes he has the

strangest ideas."

She set her cup back on its saucer.

"I like Uncle Bill," I said. "He's nice."

"He *is* nice," she said. "I missed him a lot when I lived in California."

"I know," I said.

When we finished our tea, we washed the dishes, then set them on a wooden rack to dry. I was worn out by the things that had happened that day, so I went to bed early. Lying there, I looked out my window, at houses silhouetted against the sky, rows of stonework chimneys leading to a steep cliff that lined the valley. I thought for a while of Kelly, how beautiful she was. And of Tommy, how an anger burned within him. Most of all, though, I thought of my mother. Again I remembered what Old Patterson had said, that I was a guest in this country, a remark that made me feel unwanted and misunderstood, which I finally knew was how my mother must've felt while she lived with us in the States. She was a tall, quiet woman strong enough to leave home, strong enough to return.

By the time the Christmas holidays arrived, I was seeing Kelly again: we sat in my uncle's nursery; we went to the milkbar; we walked to Miller's news agency, where we bought the *Morning Herald* simply for the comics and the movie page. At school, I finished my two weeks' detention and was free to play rugby again, but Tommy never joined us. He sat alone in the parking lot, except on those days when Jeannie joined him there. At home, I felt a distant melancholy settle between me and my mother. I noticed the great interest she showed in old manuscripts, how she began to wear gray and even black, and how at dinner she ate less. I have often thought of how pretty she looked on the night I walked home alone, as she sat at our kitchen table, wearing one of her new Grace Brothers dresses, neither of us understanding we had arrived at a crossroads, a place where our paths would slowly move apart, mine leading toward school and women, hers bringing her more deeply into the country she again called home.

THE AUSTRALIA STORIES

MY GRANDFATHER

My grandfather was a free settler; that is, he was not a convict. He came to Australia because his family did not have much land. For a while, he built stonework houses, then after the economy turned bad, helped build the Sydney Harbour Bridge. The Sydney Harbour Bridge is a beautiful piece of architecture: sandstone pillars at either end, the bridge itself a bronze arch, the road passing along the bottom. Because of its shape, locals call it "the coathanger." He worked six days a week, first on the foundation and later spot welding. On Sundays, he went to First Anglican for the nine o'clock service, then spent his afternoons in the yard, trimming the lawn with a small pair of hand clippers because a lawnmower was an unnecessary expense.

My grandparents had two children, a boy and a girl. They both attended the Christian Brothers School, were baptized in the Anglican faith, and brought up to believe in the official history of Captain James Cook and of Governor Arthur Phillips. Australia, at that time, was a wide open space, the bush, the black stump, the end of the civilized earth. Its main exports, wool and minerals. Its population, less than five million. Its one dream, to come into its own so that its citizens might be made whole again. Above my grandfather's bed hung both the cross and a picture of Queen Elizabeth, as if the two, in his mind, were equally important.

After finishing the Harbour Bridge, my grandfather had difficulty locating work, even part-time or what he called casual labor. For a while he worked as a carpenter's assistant and later as an interior painter, but by then he drank most nights, Bitters his favorite beer. The days he spent in his bedroom, the curtains drawn, his life bankrolled by the dole. The nicest thing he ever did: he gave my mother money for the trip to

America so she could be with my father, Robert Browne. The meanest: he forbade her from dating her first love, an Aboriginal man of mixed blood.

My grandfather spent his final days walking along the North Heads. There has always been speculation about his last years—why he moved north, why he did not try to win back my grandmother—but my opinion is this: he wanted to walk along the shore, looking out to the Pacific, and remember the land of his childhood. When he was seventeen a ship brought him from England to Sydney; he married at nineteen, had two children, worked for years, lost almost everything by the age of fifty. The only visible remains of his life, a few houses he helped build in the western suburbs and the impressive bridge that connected the two halves of the city. He died in bed, June 14, 1972, his hands folded neatly across his chest, his eyes already closed, his liver no longer able to support a man of his habits. Beside his bed, *The Book of Common Prayer*. On its first page, an inscription, "To my large-hearted son who always placed his hopes in the colonies—love, Mum."

MY GRANDMOTHER

My grandmother descended from convicts. Convict lineage is now a mark of pride among many Australians, though it was not always that way. She rarely spoke of her own grandfather—a Welshman sentenced for pickpocketing—except to say he had a fine sense of humor and came good in the end.

My grandmother, herself, was born in the Blue Mountains. The Blue Mountains are an hour west of Sydney—sharp granite peaks forested with gum trees so thick they give off a light blue haze. She attended a one-room bush school up through Year Six. After Year Six, she helped her mother, who worked as a seamstress. During the day, my grandmother sewed woolen jackets and ankle-length dresses—she was particularly gifted with lacework—and in the evenings, she read by herself: *The History of British Kings*, *Bleak House*, *Jane Eyre*, *Pride and Prejudice*. She loved histories, romances, and almost anything to do with England.

When my grandmother was sixteen, she met my grandfather, a man who ventured into the mountains only to help build the old May Cottage in the township of Katoomba. The May Cottage overlooked the Jamison Valley—the gum trees, the streams, the ancient stone pillars. My grandfather built two stone fireplaces and two stone chimneys, neither of which are still present today, but which were considered exceptional during his time, fine English stonework, a good eye for arrangement, careful overall design. My grandmother was taken with him—his blue eyes, the turn of his accent, his diligence and handiwork. His first words to her: "How does a bloke keep the bloody mossies off himself on a day like today." His second: "If you don't mind me noticing, Miss, you're prettier than any of the girls I knew back in London."

They were married six months later, my grandmother believing they'd one day move to England and start a family. My grandfather wanted to return home, money filling his pockets, and buy a small house. He pictured himself as a man who migrated to the colonies, then returned a success. The twist to their tale is summed up in two words: the Depression.

After my grandfather could no longer find work as a stonemason, he took government work building the bridge. My grandmother raised produce in her garden:

mandarins, kumquats, tomatoes, and cauliflower. By now, her two children, William and Sarah, had been born, their hands attached to the hem of her skirt as she stood at the farmers market each Wednesday, selling fresh fruits and vegetables. Each week, they were lucky to leave with enough money to buy fish or a small chicken.

It was during this period, everyone figures, that my grandmother developed her interest in horticulture. The lawn, which my grandfather cut every Sunday, was gradually replaced by rose bushes, petunias, snapdragons, and when the Depression was over, a sandstone birdbath and patio table. Spanish roses corkscrewed up through the trellis; tulips emerged each spring; alyssum blossomed white as snowcover along the ground. It was all terribly English, everyone said. A rose garden. A tea garden. A place fit for the Queen.

It was as though she were preparing herself for her life overseas—an English life, a Welsh cottage, perhaps a Cornish country home. That life, however, never emerged. There was the Depression, the children, the Second World War. In photographs from the 1950s and 1960s, my grandmother appears hopeful, then distanced, and finally removed. The plants in her backyard gradually changed from roses to wattle, from watercress to waratahs, from an English to an Australian sensibility. She filled the ground with plants locals called "natives," but late one May, my grandparents lost their house to the bank, the two of them retreating to a two-bedroom unit they rented from a man who'd also worked on the bridge.

The rest is not difficult to understand. My grandmother had a growing fondness for Sydney, for the Blue Mountains, for the state of New South Wales itself. At night, she no longer read Dickens or Austen, but instead works of local history: *Australia, Our Home* and *The Founding of a Southern Nation*. My grandfather continued to drink, selecting a pub where other men like himself gathered, men who'd left England only to find a disappointment too great to carry home. At this time my grandmother began to write: essays on her experience at the bush school, a memoir of the Blue Mountains, one chapter beginning "As the granddaughter of a convict, I have the burden of isolation, the longing to be reunited with England, but only now, as an aged woman, can I see the foolishness of such desire." She was not able to publish her work during her lifetime. Many original pages have gone missing. After she finished writing the essays about her youth, she decided to leave my grandfather and return to the mountains, where she bought a small cottage not far from where she met him. His two stone chimneys were still standing then, finely crafted monuments to his earlier life, though they would soon be torn down.

She spent her final years leading public bushwalks into the valley of her childhood—down the Giant Stairway, past the stony Three Sisters, past Sublime Point, on toward Wentworth Falls. She showed visitors how to make bush-devils; she pointed out wallaby dens, rosella nests, places where the Aborigines once walked. At night, she made campfires: she grilled snaggers and onions; she made billy tea in a large metal pot; she bedded down beneath a canopy of gum trees, the electricity of stars her only light, her dreams of merry old England a distant memory, nothing more than a silly girlhood desire.

During these years, my grandmother wrote her best-known essays. In them, she talks about the happiness she found alone in the mountains. "There are many things I did not know," she wrote. "I was brought up to believe a good English woman found contentment in marriage and in family, but here I am, in my own cottage, perfectly content. I have never felt so at peace as I do now. I miss my husband, I miss a family house, but I wouldn't trade what I have for any of those things." (*Bush School*, p. 23)

No one knows how my grandmother met her death: two weeks after my grandfather passed away, she simply left her house for a private bushwalk—no tourists this time, just a solo walkabout. The last person to see her, Mrs. Judith O'Neal, watched her descend the Giant Stairway and make her way east, moving slowly through the underbrush. Four days later, servicemen searched the area, discovering only her scarf and three kilometers later her hat. The police report officially listed her as missing, not dead. In the months that followed, neighbors claimed to see lights in her cottage, but the source of those lights was never found. After my grandmother's disappearance, my mother moved back to Australia and lived in that cottage for eight years.

For a while, I lived there with my mother. One warm November day, while she was reading my grandmother's essays, she turned to me, her expression heavy with thought as though she had just realized something important. She was wearing a white summer dress and eating tangerines my uncle had left in a basket at our door. "It's strange," she said, "the things a person can leave behind."

THE COTTAGE

My grandmother's cottage was a small two-bedroom house, centered on a large plot of land. It was made from wood, roofed with corrugated iron, a beautiful veranda across its front, windows opening to the east and west in such a way as to catch the sun. Inside, she had a potbelly stove as well as a stone fireplace similar in style to the ones my grandfather once built, but not as well crafted. During her final years, she painted her cottage Federation Colors—that is, green and gold—as a way of showing pride in her native land. The colors, as strange as they sound, were popular for a time, blending well with the surrounding gum trees and wattle.

Following my grandmother's death, my mother made numerous trips to Australia—summer trips, Christmas trips, a few weeks squeezed into March, trips to see my uncle and old friends, but trips mainly to visit the cottage that held the mysteries of my grandmother's life. As best she could, my mother assembled my grandmother's writings, collecting some essays into one published book: *The Bush School and Other Early Experiences*. The collection was favorably reviewed in *The Sydney Morning Herald*, earning a coveted Phillips Award for Historical Memoir, and sent back to press eight times by its publisher, MacMillan Australia, in its first year alone. Later, it was published in England, in Canada, and finally, as a small paperback edition in America, its title changed, of course, to *Outback Australia: One Woman's Tale*.

In Australia, her book was scripted into a six-part radio drama, broadcast over the ABC—the Australian Broadcasting Company—a production that proved to be one of its most popular shows that year. In it, she is depicted as an early feminist, a woman who, once her children were grown, left her husband to live by herself. In many ways, she turned her back on tradition: she made enough money to buy a cottage, she became the first female tour guide in the mountains, and she solicited the friendship of many Aborigines, mostly women. Around Sydney, she became known as "the woman who walked off into the valley and did not return." People speculated that she joined a group of Aborigines. She fell in love with Australia, they said, then with its original inhabitants, stripping off her Western adornments—her scarf, her hat—and following them out past the mighty Murray River, perhaps beyond. Shortly after the first broadcast, an anonymous person posted a sign atop the Giant Stairway, stating that my grandmother was last seen "at this spot, before she willingly traveled east with unknown Aborigines."

In the wake of its success, many Australians found an idol in my grandmother, a woman who said things they felt but were afraid to say. She questioned English rule, frowned upon the masculine code of mateship, and believed women had a great untapped strength inside themselves. At the end of one essay, she writes, "I wish I had my life to live over. I should've been strong

earlier. I should've known what was inside of me."
Here, I find her words easy to hear, easy because of
their simplicity. Though unpublished in her lifetime,
she seemed to sense that someday many people would
read her work.

Encouraged by the book's popularity, my mother
tried to assemble my grandmother's early memoir, but
large sections were missing, left behind in Sydney or
perhaps destroyed by my grandmother herself. After
three years, my mother was only able to assemble sixty
original pages. Enough for two magazine articles, not
nearly enough for a second book.

MY MOTHER

My mother was born in Burwood. Burwood, at that
time, was a growing suburb of Sydney, a place of parks,
corner milkbars, and open-air fruiters. In many ways it
was the heart of the country, a home for the growing
middle class, hemmed in by other suburbs, yet far
enough from the city to maintain its country feel. She
was given the name Sarah Anne, but most always went

by Sarah or just Sare.

As a girl, she loved to draw and play the piano. Her drawings often featured my grandmother, a woman who usually appears taller than anyone else represented, her hair falling in straight dusty strands, her eyes blue, though in reality they were brown.

When she was fifteen, my uncle led my mother into a more active social life. They had been close, children pressed together by bad times, a father taken by drink, a mother struggling with disappointment. Together they attended movies, dropped by parties, went to gatherings that were called fetes. They beached at Bondi and later Coogee, where sitting on parchment sand they could see a small plot of land, surrounded by seawater, called Wedding Cake Island, a rise with decorative white bluffs and cliffs like icing. They rode the Harbour ferry to Watson's Bay, where standing beside the water they could see, on one side, the imperial North Heads and, on the other, the Harbour Bridge. On such days, they ate meat pies in paper takeaway bags, they picnicked by Town Hall, they ducked into a bottle shop and pinched two beers when they thought they wouldn't be caught. For a while they were a family within a family, a bond based on equal parts necessity and pleasure. My uncle had an early sense of himself, that he'd never marry. My mother, however, gradually found herself enamored of the opposite sex.

On one of their excursions to Watson's Bay, my mother met a half-Aboriginal boy named Toby Broome. He worked at a milkbar that also served hot food. At first it was merely a casual relationship, the two of them talking every week or two, him in his white apron, my mother and William eating fish and chips, which later on became "compliments of the house." Not long after, she went there each Saturday because she was starting to fall for him, his eyes like coal, his face thin, his upper lip covered with the sparse hairs of an adolescent mustache. He was sixteen, having left school only three months before to apprentice himself. He lived above the milkbar, a tiny room that opened to the water, wooden crates for a bookshelf, his clothes folded neatly under his bed.

My mother fell in love slowly. She was wooed by his large gesturing hands, by the way he said "compliments of the house," and by how he looked at her when he thought she wouldn't notice. He had tender eyes. She liked his full name, Tobias, and thought that spoke well of him. When he asked her out to a movie, she accepted. It was the first Saturday in months my mother hadn't spent with my uncle. She was with Toby, downtown at a George Street cinema, while my uncle, covering for her, saw a movie across town.

After that, they saw each other every Saturday night, often meeting at Town Hall, beside the large stone columns. They kissed once, then walked to Pitt Street or perhaps to the Rocks where they wouldn't be refused a drink. On these nights he told her the secrets of his birth: he'd been born to a young Aboriginal mother, an older English father. For a while, his parents lived together, north of Sydney, in a place called Newcastle, but his mother, only seventeen, ran away one night, homesick for her own people, leaving Toby in his father's care. For two years his father searched but couldn't find her. Only then, resigned to separation, did he remarry, this time choosing an English woman closer to his own age. They continued to live in Newcastle, Toby attending a public school filled mainly with Aboriginal children, his parents sectioning off land for a dairy farm. When he was twelve, his father sent him to live with his uncle near the city. He lived there until he was fifteen and moved to Watson's Bay, where he hoped to learn about business. "Someday," he said, "I'll leave this place. Open shop elsewhere. The city's no place for a man who's half-Abo. No one particularly likes us here."

The affection my mother felt for him was a sweet, girlish affection—or so I've been led to believe—one filled with flowers and candies, letters sent through the mail, the stamp turned upside down to indicate love. They met always in the city, my uncle tagging along for an early dinner, maybe one drink, then he'd leave, taking a taxi up to the Cross or perhaps to Luna Park, where he'd meet friends. My mother, however, always stayed in the city, charmed by its lights, its gardens and artwork. Toby was her protector, her love. They planned to tell their parents, planned to marry, but must've sensed, even then, that their families would disapprove and that the pressure would divide them. Even Toby's father, when told, would look away: "Such a thing," he'd say, "will only bring you sorrow."

My grandfather was drunk when he found out. He walked around the house, yelling, "I'm a bloody stupid man—bloody stupid to let things get this far." My grandmother stood up to him in a rare demonstration that none of them, not even my mother, would understand for years. "Stupid, yes," she said. "Stupid because you don't know the value of love. You no longer have the decency to hope for anything, except another schooner of beer. I can only hope Sarah's life ends up better than mine."

After this, they arranged secret meetings in the city, but slowly my mother lost her joy in it, not being able to please both her father and Toby. She spent many afternoons crying in her room, her head supported by a damp pillow. Toby, too, must have felt this sorrow because he let her leave him so easily. After the night she did not meet him in the city, he only sent two letters: the first asking her to run away with him, the second saying he would soon finish his apprenticeship and leave. My mother didn't return either letter, but kept them in her jewelry box, the lined paper yellowed, Toby's slanted handwriting difficult to read, a certain carefulness in the tone as if he'd drafted each letter many times.

Afterward my mother fell into a depression. She went to school. She spent evenings at home. Occasionally she went out with my uncle, but she was never again allowed curfew past nine o'clock. After my mother finished her schooling, she worked at a fabric store, following the family tradition of sewing. Only at the age of nineteen did she venture again into the city at night. She no longer went to Watson's Bay or even Town Hall, but wandered around the Cross with my uncle. She met my father in 1964, toward the start of the Vietnam War. He was an American, on R and R. They met on the second day of his leave. This time, she was not slow to fall in love. Not slow at all.

A MISSING SECTION OF

MY GRANDMOTHER'S MEMOIR

One of the missing sections resurfaced years after my mother tried to find it: it was found slipped into the stuffing of a Queen Anne chair, which Mr. Cheeseman, a Blue Mountains antiques dealer, had purchased from my grandmother's estate. On local talk radio, he explained how he'd discovered it: "It was a bloody strange thing. It really was. I was stripping back this old chair, when I sees this envelope in with the stuffing. I pulls it out and find out it's typing, a good twenty pages at that. I didn't think much about it at the time, not until I sees the daughter again in town. I tells her I found this typing, and that's when I know it's valuable. I reckon it's about the woman who went a-walking. The one who was never seen again."

This missing section is, in some ways, a departure from the strong, overly moral woman depicted in the early writing. My grandmother emerges as a woman in need of love and unsure how to find it. Her parents, by now, have passed on; her husband is unavailable because of drink. She spends the majority of time in her garden—the roses, the annuals, the small fish pond. She has yet to fill the ground with Australian "natives." Likewise, she has yet to question her role as a wife, as a woman, as an English mother. She sits beneath a jacaranda, its violet blooms in season, when the nursery deliveryman enters her yard, a Turkish immigrant named Yasar Hasim. He carries two sacks of peat moss, two more left on his cart outside. For the first time she offers him a cup of tea. It is an odd gesture for my grandmother, one that must have been preceded by days of thought.

The manuscript is unclear on many significant details about Yasar's life. We merely know this, that his family emigrated from Turkey, that he lived in Sydney for ten years, that he was not married nor did he care to be. He simply enters as the large-shouldered deliveryman for Thompson's Nursery, a man who dropped in on Tuesdays, again on Fridays. My grandmother's own words tell it best:

> Twice a week, I wonder at his body, at the sheer beauty of it. He comes in through the side gate, wearing a nice long-sleeved shirt and pressed khaki pants. He has the most pleasant disposition of any man I've ever known. He sets my purchases by the veranda and sits with me for an hour or so, drinking tea and looking out over my garden. In Turkey, his family was employed as gardeners. "The roses are good this year," he tells me.
>
> "I'm glad you think so," I say.
>
> "Roses are very hard to grow here," he says.
>
> "That's what makes them so beautiful, all the hard work."

He considers this for a long while, sitting there with his tea saucer balanced in his palm. I have seen this expression many times, his mind in deep contemplation. I learn what I've learned before, that his wisdom is not like my own, that his family is from Turkey, mine from England. "That's the funny thing about the English," he tells me. "They all want Australia to be England. Australia is not England. It is not Turkey. It is only Australia. It cannot be anything else." (Manuscript, pp. 21-22)

My grandmother, by this point, is broken-hearted. She will never migrate to England. Her husband has left her bed and, most nights, chooses to drink with his mates. Her children will soon leave home. It is under these conditions that this man enters, that he is offered tea, that he is scheduled to bring deliveries *every* Tuesday and Friday. My grandmother had planned, one can assume, to have a distant courtly relationship, with only hints of sublimated romance. What she got, however, was something else entirely.

Yasar Hasim met her on Tuesdays, on Fridays, sometimes on Mondays as well, often bringing cut flowers or a particularly nice seedling ready to bloom. They met in her backyard, at the nursery and once at the Royal Botanical Gardens, which overlooks the Harbour. "It is so strange," she wrote, "to see both the Bridge and Yasar in the same afternoon. It's a sacrilege, a sweet, undeserved blessing. I've lived too long in the confines of our 'culture.' I've been a daughter, a wife, a mother. Rarely have I allowed myself such luxury, except of course for my garden. I've spent too little time thinking about myself and love. In these things I find true joy." (27)

My grandmother had not expected to find attraction so deeply knotted inside her. She had not known love could make you want a person so desperately. Each detail reveals her emotions for him: "He has lovely large hands, thick-fingered and dark" (19) and "His eyes, I must admit, are unfathomable, and though I understand our afternoons must eventually end, I cannot help but look into them. They make me feel stronger than I have ever felt before. With him, I sense there is a life inside of me, one I am slowly learning to live." (32)

He moved into her life like thunder, and through

his presence, she was able to reshape her own life, slowly and through a keen understanding of both herself and her upbringing. At this point her narrative rhythm changes, becomes freer, picks up a lighter vocabulary. As a young woman, her understanding of Australia was tainted with convict overtones. But now it opens toward a new Australia:

> It is amazing that his family has overcome in ten years what my family has not accomplished in three generations. He doesn't thirst for his old country the way I did. He doesn't live within the elaborate rules we've made for ourselves. On walks, he identifies native plants for me. The waratah, gravillia, silver gums, a violet creeper. He picks up seeds and calls them by their common names: a gumnut, a gooseberry, a bush-devil. A bush-devil, I've learned, is a small round seed, a face really, complete with horns and eyes and pointed nose. For me, the whole country expands, filling itself with mystery. I'm a Commonwealth citizen, but the life I now long for is a new life. I'm too old to be falling in love with a man, a country, and myself, but I

am. I don't know how to stop, but already I see the danger. (31)

In April 1967, my grandmother leaves my grandfather, both of them citing unresolved difficulties as the official reason for divorce. She gathers her belongings into two trunks, allocating the rest to the Salvation Army, or *the Salvos* as they were called. She boards the three-thirty train that will take her past Paramatta, past Lidcombe and Emu Plains, until she arrives at Katoomba, not more than 100 meters from where, as a girl, she used to buy rock candy and licorice. She takes a part-time position as a seamstress. On her days off, she walks through the valley, learning more plant names—blue gum, spiny fern, lemon shoot—until her mind is an encyclopedia, her heart opening to the only thing that will fill it, the presence of the land itself, the sky, the trees, the water that runs through it. She's happy here, happy in a way she had not known she could be. She writes of a satisfaction often hidden from women, the pleasures of a solitary life. When she's sixty-three, she becomes the first female tour guide in the mountains, leading public expeditions into the Jamison Valley, perhaps beyond. She's allowed three more years before she finally walks down the Giant Stairway, Mrs. Judith O'Neal spotting her along the way, and is swallowed up by rocks and leaves until only her hat and scarf remain.

It goes without saying that Yasar Hasim didn't join her in the mountains. Years before, he was offered a job in Melbourne, where a different Royal Gardens awaited him, its land colder, its soil darker, a small gardener's unit his for the asking. After the missing manuscript was uncovered, Mr. Ed Horner from the Historical Society traveled to the Melbourne Gardens to find him. Yasar Hasim had died three years earlier, the only trace of my grandmother found ironically in a hybrid rose he had developed. It bore her middle name.

THE RISE OF A NATION

In the mid-1700s, the English understood that a Great South Land existed beyond the equator, down deep into the Pacific, where the water was turquoise and rough. Like most famous explorers, Captain Cook was not the first, but his arrival occurred at an opportune time. He charted the coast, surveyed the shore, and claimed the continent for King George III. New South Wales, it was called, soil thick with vegetation, water teeming with life, inhabited by natives who, in Cook's own words, appeared "far more happier than we Europeans." Cook returned to England with the information that the South Land was not an island of wealth, but one of rich soil and simple life. In the end, though, the continent was designated as a penal colony, the first prisoners transported a few years later.

My earliest Australian ancestor, my great-great-grandfather, was sentenced to seven years for pick-pocketing. By all accounts, he was a small man, barely over five feet tall, gentle hands, a face that blended easily into crowds. He was caught in Piccadilly Circus, his fingers stretched into the pocket of a man who, when uniformed, was a constable. He did not fare well in Australia, damp weather claiming his life just six months after the completion of his sentence. His one footnote in history: he helped run the first stagecoach line between Sydney and Newcastle as part of his forced daily labor.

My great-great-grandmother fared much better. A convict herself, arrested for petty theft, she became a much-admired seamstress, a skill she was able to pass along to her daughter and grandchildren. My grandmother also started as a seamstress, her afternoons spent in her mother's shop, but eventually other things interested her more: gardening, reading, trying to find a life of her own.

Here I see the first indication that my grandmother would be the person she became: she descended from a line of strong, determined women. She could not have known about her posthumous success, but each time I read her book, I think she must have sensed it. Her best essays read like letters, a wise woman revealing what she has learned. She critiqued the government, business structures, and social customs; she criticized the nation's treatment of the Aborigines. "My biggest regret," she wrote, "was that I believed the lie. I believed we, as English, were somehow better than other people, but now I see how this belief limited me in so many ways." In the end, though, she was best remembered for her advice to women, that they shouldn't be afraid of leading their own lives, that happiness wasn't limited to marriage, and that strength often came from being alone.

THE BLUE MOUNTAINS

When my mother was nineteen, she followed my father, Robert Browne, to America, where I was born. I had a good childhood, but I knew even then that my mother was not happy and regretted leaving her family. She checked the mailbox regularly; she called home every other weekend; some days she would drive to the Pacific and look across it, her eyes scanning the horizon, where water curved around the earth and, some seven thousand miles later, connected with Australia.

After my grandmother's death, my mother returned to Sydney many times, and in 1979, decided to stay for good, claiming as her inheritance my grandmother's mountain cottage. She took a job at the Historical Society where, along with her other duties, she edited my grandmother's essays for publication. The missing chapters, perhaps four in all, were never found, though my mother searched diligently, only to uncover numerous notes and a partial draft of Chapter Six. It begins:

> I am a woman in Australia, and that, I've always thought, is a difficult thing to be. Since its beginning, Australia has formed itself on the idea of mateship and other alliances between men. The place of women is relegated to the home, to the children, to the backyard garden. For years I've wanted to step beyond this, but did not know how, perhaps still don't, but staying in such a small space is a failure I'd rather not accept. I'd like to think this is my own personal failure, but as I look around I see other women who have failed like me. (Uncollected works, 8)

From here, the draft wanders into notes and other unrelated ideas, as well as a partial outline that connects some of the chapters my mother was able to find.

For a while, my mother collected these notes into a binder, including even old grocery lists and little reminders. Many of them deal with the deliveryman Yasar Hasim, which led my mother to believe that the manuscript found in the chair was one of the last essays completed. Other notes focus on her children and her job. The most haunting note, however, is written to my grandfather years before she left him: "Someday I will walk away and no one will find me. I will simply go into the country and will not come back." Most likely this is a response to one of his drinking binges, but still the words hold a dark prophecy, as if she'd carried this idea for years.

For months my mother reviewed the known chapters, looking for ways to edit them into a second book. She interviewed my grandmother's friends; she reviewed old correspondence; she spent her evenings at the Historical Society. Her own letters to me from the early 1980s betray what she most wanted, to have known her mother better. In them, her voice begins to take on the tone and vocabulary of my grandmother. Once she wrote, "I continually notice how Australia is predicated on the idea of male companionship, leaving women to form their own social attachments." Other people, too, noticed how her voice deepened and adopted an unfamiliar timbre. She began wearing clothes slightly outdated, and that spring, she paid local boys to repaint the house green and gold, though that color scheme had fallen out of style many years ago. She thought of herself, I'm sure, as "the daughter of the woman who went a-walking," indicating, at least to me, that she'd already begun to blur the line between herself and her mother, to mix generational divides, which can be a dangerous thing.

In town, people often asked her how the new book was going. "Fine," my mother would say because, by then, she'd started to know my grandmother's life through personal repetition. She'd walked the mountains long enough to understand bush-devils and Wentworth Falls, to know the secret grooves in the Giant Stairway and the hidden wallaby dens. She interviewed Mrs. Judith O'Neal, the local servicemen who searched for my grandmother's body, even Aboriginal women who taught my grandmother about bush food and the mythic Dream Time.

In July 1987, fifteen years after my grandmother's disappearance, my mother set out to reenact the famous walk down the Giant Stairway—into the valley and off through the underbrush, along the same trail where the hat and scarf were discovered. "It is here," she wrote in her pocket diary, "that I feel closest to my mother. Clouds rise out of the valley and collect above us, leaving us a clear view of the gum trees and peaks. The cliffs are colored like steel, some rocks darker where water flows over them." She was accompanied by an Aboriginal man named Glenn Matthews, who, it turns out, was a distant nephew of my mother's old love, Toby Broome.

They walked along old hunting trails, east toward Bathhurst, then over the rocky precipice of Johnson's Bridge, my mother wearing clothes similar to those my grandmother wore: a white blouse, a woolen jacket, khaki pants. At the appropriate place she leaves a scarf then later a hat, noticing their odd placement. "It is the saddest thing to walk this trail," my mother writes, "knowing I lost my mother here, but I feel very close to her. I've wanted it for years, this closeness. I've searched for it on every page she left me, but did not find it. Unknowingly, she gave her love to the world and by doing so withheld it from me."

At night, they sleep in separate tents, my mother and her guide, their bodies cocooned in down-filled sleeping bags, as it is winter in Australia. Mist settles in the valley each night, and with it comes a harsh, penetrating cold. "I haven't considered the true force of the elements," my mother writes, "the sheer isolation caused by the wind and mist. With only a thin woolen jacket, my mother was surely walking off to her own death. There's no other means of escape, unless one looks to the forgotten Aborigines or perhaps some friend she might've met along her way."

On the third morning, my mother's guide wakes to find her missing, her tent empty, her sleeping bag gone. He searches the valley all the way down to the river, but finds no sign of her, aside from a few footprints, some broken twigs, a bird that circles one or two kilometers to the south. "Now that we're so close to returning," she writes, "I know I've cheated. I cannot truly know what my mother knew because she journeyed alone. Seeing all I've seen in these past few days leads me to believe my mother resides in a place of great separation. She was able to see with such clarity because she removed herself from society. Only by myself can I feel her connection with the valley and to herself."

I'm certain my mother did not intend to depart for good, only to step into the realm of my grandmother and then step out again, but the sad facts are these: my mother died an estimated two days later, six kilometers from their field camp, her body hidden by ferns. Experts believe she wandered in a large circle before finally collapsing near a pond, her hands clutching the small pocket diary she had not written in since the day she left her tent.

Around the mountains, some say my grandmother's spirit finally descended on her. Others say she just went mad. I am not sure what to believe. I know only this: I lost my mother in that valley, in a section much farther east than my grandmother most likely traveled. Her body was recovered one week later, airlifted out on a stretcher, her heart already still, her eyes holding a measure of curiosity, as though in the final moments of hypothermia the world opened and relinquished the knowledge she most wanted.

THE GIANT STAIRWAY

I was nineteen when my mother died. I'd just started college and was living with my father. After divorcing my mother, he married and divorced again, and was right then thinking about love for a third time, but it never happened. Eventually he slipped into retirement, his days spent reading and attending veterans' functions. His love for my mother had been too great to be replaced: he'd been an infantry man on R and R, down in Sydney, drafted into a war he didn't support, she a small-town girl. Both of them needed love for reasons that, years later, turned out to be incompatible.

My father and I don't talk about her much, though she's with us. On long June days, I occasionally catch him staring into his backyard, where jacaranda trees display gossamer blossoms and scrub jays dart through the air repeating their songs. I understand he's thinking of her and of some greater happiness he was never to get beyond. Happiness has its own legacy, as does longing. There are many types of exile in the world, and most of us have a penchant for at least one.

On that cold winter's eve of 1987, after my mother's tour guide returned to town, a rescue crew was dispatched with dogs newly trained for such emergencies. Experts examined the campsite. Planes crossed the sky, one of which spotted her sleeping bag abandoned by an unmapped pond. Crews located her body, on Tuesday at 5:45, just as the sun dipped below mountain peaks, draining light from the valley and replacing it with ice. The headline in *The Sydney Morning Herald* read: "Daughter Follows Famous Mother to Her Death."

I come from a family of strong, expansive women—women who hope for what they don't yet own and have hearts too tender to absorb the loss inevitable in this life. My grandmother wanted to change her world, and in ways, she did. At the age of sixty-seven, she walked into the valley, and a few days later, her body transformed into nothing more than air and light; the person most mesmerized, my mother, could never shake the image from her mind. Fifteen years later, long after leaving my father, she retraced this journey, her spirit a custodian of history, though history didn't grant her the same mythic grace it had my grandmother, leaving her body to be discovered by modern search techniques, after which it was cremated, the ashes spread over the valley, near Wentworth Falls, which was where, weeks before, she'd intended to travel.

Years later, while visiting Australia, I returned to the Blue Mountains and stood atop the Giant Stairway. The valley stretched as far as I could see, long and narrow, commemorating ancient glacial progressions, the floor thick with gum trees, their withered limbs supporting clusters of leaves and, every now and then, the white plumage of a cockatoo. I didn't descend the steps, feeling I was no longer entitled, but merely looked. I singled out streams and distant boulders, I heard the sorrowful laugh of the kookaburra and, a few minutes later, the sound of a woman who, projecting her voice, waited for its return.

That afternoon I left the stairway, sadness settling like a stone within me. I believed, even then, that I might not visit the mountains again: the last of my family, my uncle, had moved to the suburbs two years before. I had a girlfriend I loved and a retired father, both of whom lived in America. I looked back only once, seeing trees sewn together and cliffs like cut glass. I was completing the last part of the journey, the part my mother and grandmother could not accomplish, walking up the poorly paved road that connects the Stairway to the township of Katoomba, passing familiar milkbars and pie shops, then finally the green and gold cottage that years ago was sold. I was returning, but returning, I've found, is a lonely act. It's another way of starting over.

A CHRISTMAS MEMORY
1979, 1989

The Thursday before Christmas, we took the train to the city. For hours, my mother and I walked through shops. She wanted a video recorder. I wanted a bike and a handheld video game. We looked at these things, displayed in department stores, but didn't buy them. Instead, my mother bought me new shorts and a pair of shoes.

Afterwards, we walked down to the Quay and ate fish and chips by the water. Sitting there, my mother appeared content with herself, two Grace Brothers bags leaning against her chair. We watched ferries move across the blue and disappear behind the Opera House. When we'd finished eating, she told me none of this had been here when she'd been a girl. "Not the Opera House, not these restaurants. Only the bridge." I couldn't picture the Harbour without the Opera House, those large white arcs set against the sea, but then I couldn't picture my mother as a young girl either.

As we walked up George Street, we stopped to look at window displays. Even though Christmas was a summer holiday, many shopkeepers decorated their windows with traditional snow scenes: styrofoam snowmen and paper snowflakes hung with wire. In one window, children were sledding down a slope covered with cotton batting to meet Santa dressed in a thick red coat. We laughed at how ridiculous it was to think of snow in summer. "People are rarely happy where they are," my mother said.

Eventually, I started to feel homesick. For the first time in months, I wanted to be back in California, where it would be cool and rainy and where my father would light a small fire in our fireplace. But I didn't say anything because my mother liked being in Australia. She was happy here, and I didn't want to take that from her. For the rest of the afternoon, we shopped for my uncle, eventually buying three silk ties, along with two books on gardening.

On Christmas morning, after my uncle opened his

box of ties, he held each up to his neck. "I'm the only nurseryman in Australia who wears ties," he said.

"You like wearing ties," my mother said.

"Indeed I do."

My mother seemed pleased with her gifts. I'd given her some books she wanted: a field guide to plants, another on walking trails. As for me, I got a new tape recorder so I could send letter-tapes to my father, as well as one of the handheld video games I'd wanted.

Later that day, we sat in the sun and had cold drinks as my uncle made a small fire in the barbecue pit. We grilled snaggers and onions, and while they were cooking, my mother and uncle tried to teach me an old drinking song they'd learned as kids, called "The Cockies in the Tree," but I never quite got the hang of it. For dessert, my mother brought out both Christmas pudding and pavlova. We stayed there until night, when stars appeared across the sky. By now I could find the Southern Cross, as well as a few other constellations.

When we were inside again, my uncle uncorked a bottle of wine. He played records and danced with my mother. He knew many songs from the fifties and sixties, especially those performed by harmony groups.

"This here," he said, "is one of my absolute favorites." Then he dropped the needle on "Johnny Angel," performed by Shelley Fabares. When it was over, he announced, "And now, another of my all-time *favorites*," which turned out to be the Beach Boys' "Fun, Fun, Fun." In truth, every song was one of his favorites, and for some reason, we laughed each time he said it. "I think we've heard enough of this old rubbish," he'd say when a song ended. "If you give me a moment, I'll select one of my favorites." Then winking at us, he'd flip through his 45s.

We took turns dancing with my mother. They taught me how to do the swing, the swim, and the pony, which my mother remembered doing as a girl. They even let me have a glass of wine, which didn't taste as bad as I thought it would. Much later, when the house was finally cool, we collapsed on the sofa and they started singing that drinking song again. Each time they hit the chorus, the part about cockies sitting in the tree, I tried to join in until they grew tired of singing and stopped.

As we sat there, the quiet sounds of night around us, I felt better than I had in months. We were perfectly happy, snuggled shoulder to shoulder on an overstuffed couch, as moonlight slipped in around us. At midnight, my uncle tipped more wine into my mother's glass, then secretly offered me a little more as well. "Now, Sparrow," he said, "mum's the word on the wine."

"Sure," I said.

He made a toast to commemorate my mother's first Christmas back in Oz, then another because I was there too. With that, we touched glasses and drank. I thought I should say something, but couldn't find the right words to express how I felt. Or rather, I couldn't find the right words to express what I was learning just then, that my mother somehow belonged here, in this city so far from my father, that she'd never again live in Los Angeles, in that other city I still thought of as home.

Ten years later, I thought of this day on another Christmas morning, as Taylor and I opened stocking gifts we'd given each other. Taylor and I would eventually marry, but back then we were in our young twenties, still dating. It was a crisp, California morning, rain ticking against the roof of my rented townhouse, a fire crackling in the fireplace. We were sitting on the couch, in our PJs and robes, torn pieces of wrapping paper around us, when I took the last gift from the toe of my stocking. I unwrapped it to find a Christmas ornament fashioned like the Sydney Opera House. The gift surprised me. It would've been very difficult to find an ornament like this—here in California.

"I love it," I said.

"I didn't know if you would."

"Of course I do." I looked at her, sitting on the sofa, her hair pulled back into an early-morning ponytail. "Where did you find it?"

She smiled, unwilling to tell me.

All day I noticed it, the white arcs against the green of my artificial tree. I felt a hopefulness descend on us, a sensation I didn't expect, and I started to believe that she knew what was truly important to me. I was finishing a college degree in English, and Taylor was studying for her accounting exams. The following year we would have our first real jobs: I would work at a high school, Taylor at a bank.

We spent the day at my house, watching TV and doing our best to cook a small turkey. At night, as we lay on the sofa, I told Taylor about that Christmas in

Australia. I told her that my uncle cooked snaggers and onions for our holiday meal and that afterwards we all danced to 45s. She looked at me with warm interest, an openness that years later would fade away. But I didn't know that on our first Christmas together, as I lay beside her, trying to construct stories that would explain my life, so that she would know how I became the person I was just then.

SMOKE
1994

Perhaps this would be the place to start. With my marriage. Or rather, with how it ended. My wife's name was Taylor, and she worked as an accountant for Hodgeman-Alexander. She was a tall, slender woman with a stubborn streak. I'd loved her for six years, three of which we'd been married. We had many problems, so it's not easy to say why we finally separated. I do know this: it had to do with Jeffrey Branch and perhaps other men at her company. I don't believe she had an affair. She was a loyal woman, though also committed to her own idea of a good life. Just what this life included, I didn't fully understand, but sensed over the previous year that it might not include me. Once, four months before our separation, she told me: "It's not like I haven't had opportunities to be with other men."

"Like with whom?" I asked.

"Like with Jeffrey Branch," she said.

"Who's Jeffrey Branch?"

"He's in Outside Promotions. He's new."

"Are you saying you want to *see* this Jeffrey Branch?" I asked.

She walked slowly around our kitchen. "No," she said. "I don't want to see him. But I did think about it. Thought it might be a way to end things between us."

"End things," I said. "Why are you telling me this?"

"Because I'd like you to understand me."

"I *do* understand you," I said.

"Then maybe I'd like you to understand yourself."

I remained at the table, looking at her. She stood by the sink, sunlight slanting in. She picked up a dish towel and held it. When the space between us grew heavy with sorrow, she bent over the sink and twisted on the tap, allowing the sound of water to break our silence. She continued to wash silverware and plates, even though we owned a dishwasher, then set them on paper towels to dry.

I know, looking back, I should've thrown something, I should've yelled or at least stormed off, but I only stood there. When she finished with the dishes, I said, "I didn't know you felt that way," and turned to walk out the door, but the opportunity for storming off had passed.

I walked, as I had after previous fights, through the local park and along a bike path that sloped down to a saltwater marsh. It was there I called my uncle—my only living blood relative, who still lived in Sydney. "It's like I said," he explained, "the bigger the fire, the more the smoke."

"This is not a time for jokes, Will," I said.

"That is not a joke. It's the wisdom of the ages."

"Don't give me the wisdom of the ages crap. You probably klepted that from some old Bogart flick."

"Some *Hepburn* film," he corrected. "You need to get these things straight. They make the movies in *your* country, after all."

"I don't give a damn about the movies," I said.

"Listen, Kid Courage, go back, see how things are. If they're bad, call me later."

In the background, I heard people milling around his nursery. "Do you have customers?" I asked.

"Only pensioners masquerading as customers, but

now that Basil's gone, I have to help them, too."

Basil, his longtime partner, had died almost two years ago. "Go help your pensioners," I said.

"You always end phone conversations with such disdain. It's very American."

"It's not American," I said. "It's just me."

For the next hour I sat among large gray rocks and felt, as I often did after fights, rather alone and somewhat of a failure. Over the past few months I'd believed Taylor and I were passing through a period of grief, a rusty turnstile positioned before a three-year wedding anniversary, but that was not true. It was only something I told myself. Later that day, I would return home, try to patch things up; however, in three months' time, we would separate, me standing somewhat pathetically on what used to be *our* front porch, the last of my clothes bundled into a cardboard box because, as we'd decided, the luggage would be hers. On the day of our fight about Jeffrey Branch, however, I didn't know these things. I simply knew I was hurting and a little angry. My wife was probably still in the kitchen, her eyes holding back tears, her beautiful black hair falling like fringe into her face. I sat there for at least an hour, as twilight settled over the shore. A golden retriever pranced up to me, sniffed my hands, then trotted away.

When I returned, Taylor was waiting for me on the couch, a cigarette in her hand, though since I'd met her, she rarely smoked. "I don't know why you go away," she said. "It makes me fume."

"I go away because you ignore me. I don't know what else to do."

"Why are you so much like all the other men I knew?"

This was the accusation I hated most, the one I could not refute, except with generalities that would not further my cause. "Why do you always say that?" I said. "I'm not like the other men. You didn't marry them."

She looked at me, as if all hope had been scraped from inside of her, leaving only emptiness, then moved so I could sit beside her on the couch. "I don't know why I get so angry," she said, "and I don't know why you leave."

"I don't know either," I said. "It's how we deal with things." At this, her eyes took on a softness, something

I hadn't seen in a long time, then she turned away. I took her hand, but slowly she withdrew it from me.

Three hours later, when I called back, my uncle said, "You should come here. Get on a plane and make a visit."

"That's the last thing I need to do," I said, "take a trip to Sydney."

"It doesn't have to be a long trip, Kid Courage. Trust me, a short trip would be fine. It'd be good for you."

"I shouldn't even take a short trip," I said.

"But it would be nice," he said, "for you. And for me, too. You could get away, and I could be with someone who remembers Basil."

"Plenty of your friends remember Basil."

"Yes, but in a campy way. In singlets and jeans shorts. Around you, he was different. Kind of classy. I like to remember him like that."

"I definitely shouldn't go to Australia," I said.

I heard him breathe, those short, shallow breaths of contemplation. "You know," he finally said, "I imagine it must be very hard to be married. Very nice, but very hard, too."

"It is," I said.

After we hung up, I walked into our bedroom and was immediately aware of Taylor's sleeping presence, her body shielded by an aura of anger and sorrow, protective emotions that, hours before, had filled our house. I looked at how she lay in bed, her body curled into itself, seeking mainly its own comfort. Even her hands were twisted into the blanket, bringing it to her chin. I believed then the thing I did not want to believe, that happiness was slipping from us, that our hearts were no longer twinned, and that these fights might be remembered only as a burden and not as part of the cement that fused us together. I angered her, and she angered me. The saddest part: we did not court each other any more, and I knew what that meant.

During my first few days in Australia, I followed my uncle from his home to his nursery and back. His nursery was not the same one he had owned when I was a kid, but a smaller one nestled in the suburbs of Sydney. He stocked a nice selection of gift plants and seedlings, ficus trees and small annuals that would bloom in window boxes. When friends visited, he introduced me as "his nephew who said he *definitely* wouldn't visit this year."

"*Shouldn't* visit," I corrected.

"*Shouldn't, wouldn't,*" he sang, "all sounds the same over the phone."

At this point, he'd walk off to tend his nursery—to line up petunias or rearrange pink hydrangeas. One day he clustered some flowering plants around a reproduction of Michelangelo's *David*, the plants brought in close so that, from a distance, customers might reasonably think it was a naked, albino man emerging from a field of greens. Often I'd stand in the cashier's shack or, if business were slow, help Susan with the watering. My uncle had hired her two months before, his first employee since Basil. Like Basil, she was good with the books, good with customers and, also like him, she had been divorced for a number of years.

"So tell me," she said while watering the seedlings, "do you find it strange to be here, you know, now that Basil's gone?"

"A bit," I said. "Did you know him?"

"Naw. But your uncle's told me a fair few things."

"Bas was a good person," I said. "A bit loud, but

most everyone liked him."

Susan considered this, looking up at conifers that shaded the nursery. "The way your uncle tells it," she said, "I figured he was just plain gaudy."

"He could be that, too," I admitted, "depending on the day."

My uncle, by then, was about finished placing hydrangeas around the statue. His eye for arrangement was not as good as Basil's, his lines too straight, his circles too round. Finished, he stood at a distance to examine his work. "I wish someone would buy that damn statue," he said. "If you're gay, it's a bad idea to have statues of naked Greek men around. People get the wrong ideas."

"The wrong ideas?" I said.

"Well, maybe not the *wrong* ideas, but ones that aren't best for business."

"You shouldn't think like that," I said. "You should have what you want here."

"If I had what I wanted," he said, "I'd definitely go out of business."

After the first few days I was able to fall into some

sort of life—a life complete with routine and work. As a teenager, I'd helped him work his old nursery, and as a college student I'd visited twice to learn about my mother after she died. During those later trips I'd become acquainted with Sydney, particularly the western suburbs. I hoped being here again would be an act of forgetting, falling by turns into a comfortable past, but that forgetfulness did not arrive as easily as I'd wanted. I knew who I was, a man who had trouble holding on to love, a man far from home who still believed distance might provide what he most needed.

Each morning we arrived just before eight and together opened the three gates that, in recent years, had been topped with barbed wire to keep out what my uncle called "the crims." We dragged out a large metal sign that read Strathfield Nursery, Now Open, so that people might wander over and take a gander. The problem was, they did little more than that. "One of these days, I'm getting a new sign," my uncle told me. "Public Gardens. See if anyone notices the difference." As we reentered the nursery, we saw a lady pulling blossoms from a hydrangea. My uncle turned to her and forced a cough. The woman, about fifty, looked at us, perplexed, as if picking flowers were regular fare at other nurseries. When she was gone, he leaned toward me. "Inbreeding," he whispered, "it's big out here."

Around ten, Susan arrived, wearing a sweatshirt and jeans. "Good-o, boys," she said before walking to the cashier's shack. On that day she wore small diamond earrings which were something I hadn't seen her wear before. My uncle noticed this, too, his eyes following her in a new way, then he turned to me, his face somewhat serious. "There's been something I've been meaning to ask," he said.

"Yes," I said.

"Well," he began, "I've known a fair lot of people, and quite frankly, most were of the married variety."

"That's more of a statement," I said.

"If you'd give me a tic," he continued, "you'd know what I was asking. I'd like to know what finally broke up your marriage."

"What finally broke us up?" I repeated.

"When a marriage ends, there's usually a defining moment," he explained, "a time when you know why it can't go on."

"If there is," I said, "I'm not sure what that was. It

was more like a series of things, all piled up."

"If you aren't positive what it was, how do you know you want to get divorced?"

"If there was such a moment," I said, "it was our fight about Jeffrey Branch. Jeffrey Branch is this guy Taylor thought she wanted to see."

"*Thought* she wanted to?"

"Yes," I explained, "as a way of ending our marriage."

"But she didn't?"

"No," I said, "not as far as I know."

My uncle considered this. "Nope, not up to snuff. You need to do better."

"Better?" I asked. "What do you mean by better?"

"If your marriage is truly over, you need to know what ended it."

"I know what ended it. We weren't very good for each other."

He simply looked at me, his features beginning to soften, as if he realized something about me I had not yet realized about myself. "I'm glad you came for a holiday," he said. "I think it will do us both a fair lot of good."

When we were done talking, he began to unload camellias from cardboard crates, six per box, and after giving them a good drink, placed them at the front of the nursery where people outside the gates could see them.

In years past, I'd wondered why he had taken up with Basil, though clearly they loved each other. Basil was a bit racy for him: he wore singlets and jeans shorts. His favorite line was "Bugger me silly." As in, "You must be joking, Miss. Two-dollars-ninety for this milk? Well, bugger me silly." My uncle displayed two photos of him, both in the living room. In one, Basil leans against a rented Jag; in the other, he sits in a friend's convertible. He was a good-time boy, a hang-out king, something my uncle called a bed body because he liked to wake up late. Years before, when I'd known his sister, we'd assembled reasonable theories— opposites attract, access to unknown worlds—but in the end I'd opted for the simplest: they needed each other. Like most people, they were somewhat afraid of the world and wanted a place to call home.

Under the shade, in what my uncle commonly referred to as "the indoor plant aisle," Susan misted ferns hung from brass hooks. "Your uncle's in rare form this morning," she said, and I saw what I had not seen since I arrived, that Susan tried to be his friend but was kept at a distance. I noticed her earrings again, and this time I understood they were for his benefit, an attempt to look what he called "more proper."

"Oh, him?" I said. "He likes being with plants."

"That I know, but before you got here, he was agro half the time."

"He's moody," I said. "My arrival has little to do with his good mood."

"Moody," she said, "that's an understatement."

She was a small woman, her face tender, her skin white with pink undertones. "So why do you stay," I asked, "when you're plagued by him?"

"Why? Most the time I like being with him."

"I like being with him, too," I said. "As uncles go, I'd give him seven out of ten."

Her eyes became thin, her features shifting into a playful reproach. "That high?"

"On his good days," I said. "You have to remember the extra points he gets for being my only living blood relative."

"So if he were to kick off tomorrow, his rating would fall to, say, a five?"

"Basically. You have to have standards."

"In my family such standards revolve around a last will." She squeezed the bottle again, misting the plants. "So has he asked you yet?"

"Asked me what?"

"I figured he would've by now." And then, after considering it, she added, "To scatter the ashes."

"He told me he scattered them already. Somewhere up in the mountains."

"Unless I'm wrong," she said, "they're in the kitchen cupboard." She looked at me with a directness that reminded me of the way my wife used to look at me— or perhaps I should say my estranged wife. "Can I ask you something personal?"

"Sure," I said, "shoot."

"Are you divorced?"

She smiled in a way meant to tell me something, but what, I didn't know. "What brought this on?" I asked.

"Curiosity, more or less."

"Didn't my uncle tell you? My wife and I separated a little over a month ago."

"My husband and I, we separated, too," she said, "but it was a fair time back."

"Are you still separated?"

"Divorced. Very easy over here. Married then not."

"It's easy in America, too," I said.

"That's the hard part—how easily everything goes away."

Across the nursery my uncle was at the top gate helping to unload a flatbed filled with seedlings. He set them on a special display rack, rows of lettuce, cucumber, pansies, and so on. The delivery boy moved quite a bit slower than my uncle, and when he wasn't looking, my uncle shot us expressions of mock irritation, his face pinched into a cartoonish mask of exasperation.

"He has a way around the nursery," she said, "which I kind of like."

"That he does," I said.

"Though," she continued, "I wish he'd loosen up around me."

But before I could say more, we were approached by an elderly man wearing a wool jacket and tie. He withdrew a small ivy plant from a plastic shopping bag, though the ivy had pretty much had it, its vine holding only two leaves. "I bought this here," he announced in a soft, apologetic voice.

"You bought *this* here," Susan said, taking the plant into her hand. She turned it and with genuine interest examined it from various angles. "So what do you think you did wrong?"

It was a question much like my uncle would ask, one that spun a customer around so quickly he didn't know what to say. "Well," he began, "there were a couple times I forgot to water it. And perhaps the place I put it wasn't the best."

"The place you put it?" she remarked.

"Yes, on me bookshelf. It seemed a fair place, except for the heating vent."

"I see," she said.

On the other side of the nursery, my uncle was still making faces the delivery boy couldn't see: crinkling his eyebrows, raising his upper lip with mock disbelief, gasping at how much he was expected to carry. I noticed that his performance was not only for us. It was also for the benefit of the seven or eight pensioners gathered by the sandstone bench. Some of them tried not to watch, but clearly they did, amused beyond belief that a grown man would carry on simply for their entertainment.

The routine continued for a short while, my uncle helping to unload the seedlings and, when he could, making quick sardonic faces, but then his antics came to an end. He smoothed back his aluminum-toned hair and shook the delivery boy's hand as if he wished only good things might come to him. The pensioners began to disperse, walking toward the front gate where, just beyond, bus stops waited as did the more distant train station. Mary, one of the bravest, stopped to wave goodbye, a gesture my uncle pretended not to see, but right before she left, he winked at her. Out of all of them, only one man brought a plant to the counter, a single tomato vine. He dropped a dollar coin into my hand, and I placed the plant into a plastic bag.

As the man left, my uncle joined us in the cashier's shack. He stood close to me so that our shoulders touched, his body smelling of earth and plants and a very expensive cologne Basil had once informed him "did not smell cheap." After the man was a good ways out the gate, my uncle said, "They come, they go, they buy tomato plants."

"Only one," Susan corrected.

"Oh, isn't it awful!" my uncle exclaimed. "They

come, they go, they buy *a* tomato plant. Life is so very hard for the wicked!"

But then the man who had purchased the tomato plant returned, its vine protruding from the top of its bag. Very matter-of-factly he said, "Good-o mates, mind if I take an extra bag. I've got a fair walk and don't think one's going to do."

My uncle extracted a single bag, pulling it slowly from its box as though the gesture might kill him.

The man fit his first bag inside the second, then said, "Ta, maties," and left.

We closed early that day, and as Susan left I watched her walk away. She had a small, slender figure, a blue sweatshirt narrowing to her jeans. Only once did she look back. She didn't appear surprised to see me leaning against a fence post, my arms folded, my eyes following her. For a moment I had a hard time believing she was thirty-two, that she had been married and divorced and now lived in a one-room flat. What I liked about her was how she walked: she walked with a certain determination, a force that reminded me of Taylor, but with a softness mixed in.

"You like her, don't you?" my uncle asked as he locked the top gate.

"Like who?"

"You know who," he said, "Susan."

"Oh, Susan, sure I like her, but I don't *like* her."

My uncle checked the lock, then looked at my face, which gave away more than I wanted. "It must be nice to be young," he said, "to be young and have attraction come so easily for you."

"I'm not attracted to her," I said. "I just like her."

We walked on to the middle gate. "I've waited a long time for attraction to overtake me again, but I don't think it will." He looped the chain through the fence, then padlocked it shut. "Here," he said, "check this."

I put the lock in my hands and pulled. "I'm not attracted to her," I said again, and then, in a slightly different tone, "This lock's pretty well locked."

"I don't mean anything derogatory by it," he said. "I wish something like that would happen for me."

At the last gate, my uncle's ruddy hands threaded the chain through the fence, then snapped the lock home. When finished, he checked each gate before he turned his face, reddened by the evening air, toward me.

"I hear you still have Basil's ashes," I said.

He did not say anything. He simply stood there.

"I hear they might be in the kitchen cupboard."

"The kitchen cupboard!" he remarked. "How tacky. Try the hall closet. Now that's tasteful."

"It doesn't matter where," I said. "I thought Basil wanted them sprinkled over the mountains."

"Yes, in a delirium he mentioned something about the mountains, but then I thought it was a pointless ritual, me up there scattering his remains. It seemed very melodramatic and rather bucolic. He wasn't a bucolic person."

"Keeping them's a pointless ritual, too," I said.

"So you see how I'm stuck," he said, "caught between two pointless rituals, not knowing which to choose."

We began walking to his car. I carried his satchel, my jacket folded over my arm. It was a typical night in Sydney, twilight dim across the horizon, the moon half-invisible above us. I was aware of all the scents around us: of the coffee shop, fish and chips, petrol fumes drifting in from the expressway. We shared the sidewalk with a number of businesspeople returning home, most wearing hats and overcoats. At a corner, I put my hand on his shoulder and said, "Maybe you'd feel better if we played out that pointless ritual and went to the mountains."

"I'm not sure I'm into feeling better," he said. "You have that expression in America, don't you?"

"What expression?"

"*Into*?" he said. "Like, you're *into* something?"

"We have it," I said. A large bus passed, releasing exhaust. "How about this," I suggested. "Tomorrow's Sunday. After work we take the one-fifteen to the mountains, and once there, you can decide."

"For a nephew, you're very pushy." As we crossed the street, his pace slowed, his hands pushed deep in his pockets. "If I went, I could make up my mind once there?"

"No pressure either way."

"I'll think about it," he said.

On the way home, he fell into a contemplative mood. From his house, we could see the city, distant skyscrapers rising like monuments to modern man, and behind them, the last purpling of dusk. We sat in his backyard drinking merlot, and listened to the chatter of magpies and cockies. By now, my uncle had started to relax, rolling his tie into his shirt pocket and unbuttoning his collar. "I don't know why things end," he said. "We live under the assumption they go on forever. It's a dangerous lie we tell ourselves."

"It is," I said.

"I mean, we project ourselves out into the infinite future, but it's a very small time we get here, isn't it?"

"Very small," I said.

Inside the house, my uncle led me to the closet where he kept Basil's urn. It was tall and turquoise, trimmed with gold. He took it out and held it in his lap. "I don't know what happens to a person, how their body withers down to nothing more than this." He tilted the urn so I could see it. On its side, it bore a picture of a lion, one that resembled a child's drawing, all circles and lines. "You realize," he said, "that Bas picked this out before he died."

"It's nice," I said.

"It's *not* nice," he said. "It's one of the most hideous, utterly woggish things he ever chose."

"It's not hideous," I said.

"If you ask me, he chose it just to torment me. He knew I'd look at it every time I needed sheets, and there, sitting next to the pillowcases, would be this god-awful lion."

"You shouldn't talk about him that way," I said.

"That way?" he exclaimed. He examined the urn again, a sadness working across his face. "He'd hate it if I talked about him any other way. We had our own life, and we both liked it."

"I understand that," I said, then laid my hand on his shoulder, his shirt damp beneath my fingers. "Are you going to go tomorrow?" I asked.

"I can choose up there?"

"Of course," I said.

"And you won't be upset if I choose not to lay poor Basil's remains among those pathetic old mountains, rotting away among blue gums and yubbos."

"Not at all," I said.

He looked at me, his eyes narrow, then he reached for my hand, closing his fingers around mine. His skin was callused, potting soil wedged under his fingernails. He lifted my hand, then put it down again. "I'll go," he said, "if you do something for me."

"What?" I asked.

"Tomorrow," he said, "I want you to tell me why you and Taylor really separated."

I put my hand on his shoulder. "How come you rarely let people see the compassionate side of you?"

"Because," he said, "a man needs to have style."

At one the next day, we closed the nursery and walked down the street to the train station, leaving a group of well-dressed pensioners sitting at the bus stop out front. Disregarding posted hours, Sunday 10-1, my uncle often kept the nursery open to three, even four, allowing them to remain inside, at sandstone tables that were for sale despite the fact that these same tables had been there since my last visit, three years before. It was for this reason that their faces held disappointment as they watched us leave, all of them looking as though we had betrayed them, especially Mary. At five minutes to one, she had bought one of the three remaining hydrangeas. Looking back, Susan said, "You didn't have to charge her full price, Will."

"Well, bloody hell," my uncle said, "I'll give her another free tomorrow if it will make you happy."

"It would," she said.

My uncle turned to them, his group of regulars, all dressed in their church clothes. After he had their attention, he tapped his watch repeatedly. With great exaggeration, he mouthed, "We close at one."

Seeing this, Mary began to perk up, as did two or three others, thinking my uncle might at last launch into his antics, but the only entertainment forthcoming came by way of a constable. One of the uniformed station police wanted to see what my uncle had stashed in the cardboard box.

"Holy Mother of God," my uncle said, "it's an urn."

"An urn?" the constable repeated.

"A bloody urn," my uncle said, opening the box, "for a body's remains. They're very popular nowadays. Even tacky woggish specimens like this one."

The constable stared at the lion's outline, particularly at how the lion seemed to be smiling, before stepping back and waving us through. We walked to the ticket window, where we purchased three return-trip tickets to Katoomba, then continued to Platform Number Four, where an old Lebanese gentleman sold gum, candy bars and the Sunday papers. My uncle bought *The Telegraph-Mirror*, which was the more tabloidish of Sydney's two papers. After returning, he looked at Susan and me, how we stood together, watching him.

For most of the morning, he had kept a careful eye on us, trying to decide if, in fact, we were attracted to each other. By now I was beginning to wonder myself. I had started to believe that I was just a lonely man wandering in a foreign country, a man who needed a sense of home, but as always I was not particularly good at finding this. I'd come to Australia because I wanted to remember what it was like to be a bachelor: I'd wanted to try on those clothes again, but like many things I used to own, the fit was a little tight, the legs too short, the chest narrow, the pants somewhat difficult to zip. Susan turned toward me, a gentleness evident in her, and after a moment, placed her hand on my arm.

My uncle took a seat on one of the green benches and opened the paper onto his lap. He read a few articles, then stared at twin rails stretching toward the mountains. His face was serious, and as he looked at us, it was clear he finally saw the attraction between me and Susan as nothing more than a transient emotion, a feeling that, for years to come, might possibly define my love life, flitters of hope floating away.

When the train finally came—ten minutes late—we stepped onto the last car and took the last seats. "You know," Susan said to my uncle, "you don't have to do this."

"What," my uncle said, "and be raked over the coals for going back on my word." He folded the newspaper over his knee. "I'm going to stand at Echo Point, and I'm going to see how I feel."

"Why Echo Point?" Susan asked.

My uncle leaned toward us, his face holding a new life, like a child who, after having the flu, is allowed outside for the first time in weeks. "Bas didn't say where in the mountains," he began. "Just the mountains. Across from Echo Point there's a proper garden and I believe he would like being by that." With that, he looked out the window. The suburbs sprinted past, rows and rows of brick houses, many with backyard pools, in the distance, brown fields, and beyond them, the magical plane where sky and earth merged into one inseparable line. "You know," my uncle said, "I used to feel bad about wanting to fall in love again, but I don't anymore."

"Well, good on you," Susan said.

"It's a mixed bag," my uncle said. "Years back, I thought if I kicked off first, I'd want Bas to grieve away, but that was a terribly selfish thought, wasn't it?"

"It was," I said, "but romantic, too."

"It's strange," he said, "that I can think about being in love again."

"I'm not sure I understand what love is any more." At this, Susan let her hand fall briefly against my knee.

"Oh I do," my uncle said, "it's when you see some trendy Turk, like Bas, posing next to a rented car and, two minutes after thinking, 'I'd be a fool to fall for him,' you find yourself in the passenger's seat being driven out to the beach. That's what love is," he said, "it's when things open up unexpectedly and you find your life in suddenly sharp focus again."

"I'm not sure I believe that anymore," I said.

My uncle looked at me, then rather pointedly at Susan.

Because it was clear what my uncle thought, I said, "He thinks we're attracted to each other."

"Attracted?" Susan said. She took my hand and held it, but it was more an offer of compassion than of romance. "I imagine your uncle thinks many things." She squeezed my hand once before lowering it into the space between us. "Yesterday I might have agreed, but today—well, today I don't."

"Americans," my uncle said, "are terribly brash."

"Not all Americans," I said.

"Most all. I see it on the telly, and in other Americans I've met. I saw it in your mother after she went to the States."

"I like brashness," Susan said. "It's an interesting quality."

"In ways," my uncle admitted, "but it can lead a person to believe he knows more than he does."

"Better to believe that," Susan interjected, "than to believe the other way."

Around me, I felt the air grow thick, the atmosphere taking on a certain heaviness. I heard only the sound of wheels rolling over gaps in the track and the joints between cars moving together. My uncle leaned toward me, his arms folded around the box. Beside us, windows opened to blue gums and wattle, black ash and banksia. We passed out of the suburbs and were beginning to ascend the mountains. "So give it a fair go," my uncle said to me.

"Give what a fair go?" Susan asked.

"We had a deal," he explained. "I'd drag my sorry self up to the mountains, if he told me why things went kaput back home."

"It's like he already knows," I said to Susan.

"Do you?" she asked.

"Not a clue," he said. "And it's odd I don't. I don't even know where to begin anymore."

Through the window, I could see large rocks balanced like cosmic tinkertoys, and behind them, slopes forested with trees older than anyone I knew.

"Want to know the reason my ex and I split?" she offered.

"Sure," I said. "Why not?"

"He slept with my best friend. Trashy, yet true."

"That's just it," I said. "There's no one betrayal, just all these little things that added up. I don't think either of us felt understood." I folded my hands into my lap, then unfolded them. "What I mean is this, neither of us realized how hard love could be and we weren't very well prepared for it. Do you want to know what we did our last night together?"

Susan nodded.

"We made dinner together, then she helped me pack the last of my clothes."

"She helped *you* pack *your* clothes?" she mused. "It would be nice to break up like that, very proper and civilized."

"If Bas and I were to break up," my uncle said, "I would've broken his nose. Odds are, he would've let me."

For the rest of the trip, I thought about my last night with Taylor. We made rigatoni, then sat side by side at the dinner table, me still unable to throw anything or storm off. But I didn't feel much like that anymore. She said, "I'll miss the way you make pasta. You've always been good with food." She put her hands on my shoulders, touching me gently as though she were trying to confirm our decision, that we should in fact separate, and something about that touch, as with thousands before, convinced her we were doing the right thing. If you ask me, we both knew our marriage was broken, that we'd lost something we shouldn't have lost, but neither of us knew how to go back and fix it.

In the mountains, the three of us walked down a narrow, poorly paved road that would take us to Echo Point. My uncle, a few feet in the lead, carried the box. Susan walked with me, her arm looped through mine, but I knew this gesture was nothing more than courtesy of a different kind. We passed old Victorian houses, most of which had been refurbished into bed and breakfast inns, the more elaborate ones coming right before we reached the point, their lawns neatly cut, their windows decorated with stained glass, their reader boards no longer displaying the "no vacancy" placards I remembered from my childhood. By the time we got to the valley, my uncle had grown contemplative again, his eyes holding a meaningful distance. Before us, a cliff dropped off to a stone floor. We were at one end of a glacier-cut valley, a long, narrow expanse, shaped millions of years before, carpeted with gum trees and vines—the type of sight that reminded me how small I was in the scheme of things.

We looked at the valley for a while, a beautiful scar

gouged into the earth, before my uncle stepped to the rail. "It's not such a bad place to be," he said as a breeze lifted up the cliff and chilled us.

"You don't have to do this," I said, "if you don't want to."

"Americans are very strange," my uncle said. "They talk you into doing the right thing, then try to talk you out of it."

"They're just bad with guilt," Susan said.

We watched as my uncle took the urn from the box. For a moment he stood there rather stiffly. "You know," he announced, "Bas would've been happier if his ashes were sprinkled over a Porsche dealership."

"To hear you talk," Susan said, "one wonders why you ever took up with him in the first place." She placed her hand on his shoulder, a soft, gentle gesture that caused him to relax. I saw compassion between them, an emotion they needed, but couldn't talk about, a new thing that, right then, was as shapeless and unformed as clouds above us.

"I took up with Bas," my uncle explained, "because I was terribly bad at stopping myself and doing otherwise."

With this a sadness entered him, a sadness I did not see or hear, but felt, as sure as I felt my own life. In that moment, overlooking the valley, I saw how the future would lie: Susan would stay at the nursery; my uncle would tinker with the idea of romance but in the end remain as single and celibate as a monk. In a week, I'd see Taylor again, but by then the inner workings of our love would be unmade, the cogs recalibrated, the old parts sold off to a junkyard I'd never find. On that day, I understood my sadness was not ending, but beginning, which was something I had not known until just then. I stepped to the rail, joining Susan and my uncle as he opened Basil's urn and released his remains. The wind carried the ashes far from us, lifting them toward the horizon, like smoke, until at last we could no longer distinguish them from the air, the trees, the sun.

THE LETTER
1994

I'd had my grandmother's manuscripts for two or three years before I took an active interest in them. I was twenty-six at the time, married for two years, and starting to feel alone in the world: my mother had died a while ago, my father had moved south to retire. I had my wife and friends, but that did not seem like enough. Two months earlier, my wife and I had begun to fight, and my friends, for the most part, were newly involved with jobs, caught up with promotions, paying off student loans and trying to qualify for mortgages. The following year I would be the first among my friends to file for divorce, but I didn't know that then. I was simply a young husband, trying to make an honest go of marriage, a man who was a bit lonely, though not afraid of being alone. At night I would lie in bed, Taylor beside me, and look at the manuscripts my uncle had sent me the year after the old cottage was put up for sale.

I'd read some of these pages before, when I was a kid, but was surprised at how much I'd forgotten or simply hadn't understood. On the nights when we were getting along, I'd read sections to Taylor, her body curled into mine. I'd read slowly, and sometimes I'd also read the notes my mother had penciled into the margins, cryptic messages like "Connect with Chapter Three" or "It wasn't like this at all." In other places, however, I could see evidence of my grandmother's own hand, words lightly crossed out, the name of one man, a neighbor, hidden beneath black ink.

Taylor's favorite piece was short, only two pages long, beginning with the most mundane of phrases: "Today is a day like any other." She liked it because it was casual, straightforward, not as "written" as some of the other pieces. My favorite was an untitled piece, a story held together by little other than my grandmother's voice. On the first page, I read my name—"Use for *sam* book"—but I believe she must have meant *same*. It is a thick section, eight manuscript pages long, the only manuscript coupled with a carbon copy. I like it because she wrote it late in her life, long after she was divorced. She wrote it while she was living in the mountains. One person from the Historical Society believed it may have been the last thing she wrote. In it, I finally see my grandmother, a woman who has given up on many things she believed, a woman who tried to know something about her world. She'd stopped hoping for publication but continued to write anyway.

Every time I hold the manuscript I am surprised how light it is, that old onionskin paper, each page crisp, brittle. The Historical Society once asked my mother to leave the originals, but she refused, offering instead high-grade facsimiles she herself had bound, as a gift, once my grandmother's book was published. The facsimiles were collected into three volumes: *The Bush School*, *Individual Essays*, and *Assorted Prose*. This particular piece comes from the third volume, *Assorted Prose*. Like two other late pieces, it is in fact addressed to my grandfather, but experts on historical memoir have suggested this is most likely a device, a way of helping her write, that the piece may not have been meant for him in particular. I'm not sure I believe this, but I see how it's possible, a woman without an audience trying to find one. It's more personal than most of her writing, passionate in places. She is not trying to impress, or to write "proper," as she once did. She's simply writing a note that might possibly be delivered to her ex-husband, a tangle of thoughts left behind as one of the last clues to her life. In a few months, my grandfather would die; a short time later, she would manage a final trip into the valley.

The piece begins: "I wish you could sit here with me and look at them." The "them" refers to the Three Sisters, a well-known rock formation in the Blue Mountains. A portion of this essay was published in *The Weekend Australian* on the ten-year anniversary of her book. It was excerpted in the Language section, next to an article by Thomas Keneally. In his article, Mr. Keneally refers to my grandmother as a woman who was "a fine example of female strength in old Oz, more independent and Australian than most of the blokes I know." Just below the fold, *The Australian* included a photo of my grandmother in which she is dressed in a thick flannel shirt, the brim of a horseman's hat slanting over her eyes. Her face is white, beautifully wrinkled, her cheeks lightly smudged with dirt. Her eyes are brown—a lighter brown than I remember from earlier photos. She is holding a piece of sandstone. The caption reads, "In her last years, she was fascinated with natural Australia and the tales she found there." If you look closely, you can see something rather odd: on the stone she has painted her initials—LM—in blue letters, scrawled across the flat surface of the rock. I have never known what to make of this, except for the obvious, that she was claiming pieces of the valley, leaving behind her initials, scattering them like breadcrumbs, marking the places she had traveled.

* * *

To my Gregory,

I wish you could sit here with me and look at them, these pillars of stone standing in the middle of the valley. You've seen pictures, I'm sure, how the brown rock rises in three individual peaks, each shaped the same way, the Three Sisters. Their story is simple. They were once real girls and their father, an Aboriginal doctor, turned them to stone as a way of protecting them from a tribal war. Some days I sit on a rough timber bench, at the edge of the Point, and think about that, how their story was once believed, how people looked at them and said their names: Meehni, Wimlah, Gunnedoo. I wonder if there is a thin veil between the real and the dreamtime (a fanciful thought, I know) and if we have simply chosen to live on this side of that veil, believing in Darwin and Cook and Scientific Progress. What is reality except what we make it? If we believed in a story, would that make it real?

But that is not your way of thinking, I realize. You were a man who built bridges and worked with stone. When we were young, I admired your work greatly. I would take my girlfriends to houses you had helped build and say, my Gregory built that. I would marvel at how well you fit the stones together, their smooth edges, the intricate design, how in your mind you could envision the exterior of a house, one stone connected to another, a puzzle pieced together from a quarry. I loved the way your mind worked, how your ideas were infinitely more complex than mine, how you could imagine something and then make it real with your hands. It was years before I realized that such thoughts were limiting, that there was only you and me and the things we craft ourselves, and that the rest of the world was closed to us, that we were creatures of flesh and bones and minds and not much more.

My favorite memory of you is a secret, a long-lost evening, back in May of 1958. You'd told me that you'd stopped drinking, that you were off the grog for good, and I wanted so much to believe you. Many nights you'd tell me you were going to the corner store or to Tony's, but I knew better. So one night I followed you. I trailed you down past the park, past the solid brick and tile houses, past the train station, down to the other side of Burwood, where I was sure you would duck into a pub, but you didn't go to the pub. You looked at one (the old RSL club on Matilda Street) but instead you kept walking, down George then Lindfield Lane. You never glanced back, never saw me there, wearing my good red jumper, my hair wound into a top knot, never saw your untrusting wife a block or so behind you.

I stayed with you up to Westland's Cinema, where you looked at posters and lobby cards. It was an American show called *High Seas Home*, a colour adventure starring Greg Thurman and Judy Lomar. You stared at the picture, a tall ship cutting across white water, your body bent at the knees, your hands in your pockets, your eyes transfixed. I knew what you were thinking. Of course I did. You were thinking of your own passage here, by passenger liner, the HMS *August*, a long sleek ship, three men sharing your cabin, talk of good times and fortunes moving easily among you. You were thinking of how you wanted so much from your life in the colonies, so much from a wife, a family, a job, but you never really got those things, did you?

I watched you for a minute or two, my husband hunched down to look at cinema stills, but then I was too embarrassed to look anymore. I was a poor untrusting woman. I turned and walked home, feeling bad that I had followed you in the first place. I knew you'd go back on the grog someday, but that didn't make what I'd done right. Do you remember what I did when you returned? I let the children stay outside after dark, riding their push bike up and down the street. I lit proper candles in the dining room and made you your favourite meal, chicken and cut potatoes, a dab of that rosemary gravy on the side. You never asked me why I made you a baked dinner, and I never told you. Only afterwards, when the dishes were washed and set to dry, you said, "Some days I don't know what I'd do without you."

"Only some days?"

Then you smiled at me, sitting in your old chair with its sturdy jarrah frame. You smiled for such a long time that I asked, "What's your mind all wrapped around?"

"I love you, that's what," you said.

Even now, I think if we could have held on to that feeling, if we could have shoved it into our pockets or slipped it into the thin space under our mattress, we might not have separated. If we could have felt the simple satisfaction that came from being together, we might have made our marriage last and come good again, but of course we didn't. This, I'd like to say, is one of my largest regrets, that I couldn't grow and become the person I am now and at the same time stay married to you. I've found life is an either/or proposition, and I don't like believing it must be that way.

Do you know what I did the week I left you? I never

told you. In fact I never told anyone, not Sarah or William, not even Mary who is my closest friend in the mountains. I went to every seamstress in town, trying to apprentice myself to them. Imagine that, *me*, a fifty-year-old woman, trying to apprentice myself. You must remember I'd worked as an apprentice before, my thin girlish hands hemming dresses and letting out bodices, the skin on my thumb thick from working a needle, my fingernails worn down from thimbles. I went to Strathfield and Concord, up to Lidcome and even once to Paramatta, but I couldn't find anyone to take me on, to teach my hands again how to use a needle and thread, how to work the new Singers. They looked at me, puzzled, a slight repulsion on their faces, before they dismissed me, sending me on my way back to Melanie's flat, where I slept on her sofa, a wool blanket folded over me, pictures of our children on the tea table. William had already gone off to Tafe and Sarah was in the States. Every night I thought about how far away they were—how far away you were—that I was alone, a woman with only her country, her God, and the night to hold her.

I didn't consider the mountains until the following

week. I didn't remember my mother or my father, the small, unpaved street where I met you, the mountain cottages, each with two rows of bricks for a driveway, corrugated iron slanting over the veranda, cut pieces of timber piled at the side. On Monday, I went to Linda's, where I'd worked as a girl, and found Linda's daughter, Martha, standing behind the counter. She was now a grown woman like me, a woman with four children, a husband who commuted to Blacktown twice a week. She was dressed in a smart red dress, her hair permed into curls. Her voice was louder than I remembered, a little deeper, but I could tell from her first words that she'd offer me a good wage and help me find accommodations until I'd saved enough for a cottage and a small block of land. I didn't purchase the cottage on credit. I bought it outright, almost half of my wage saved over four years, the cottage offered "as-is," which is solicitor talk for broken-down, difficult to fix up, the floorboards thin as toast.

I spent the next year working on that cottage, falling in love with it. I stripped the wood floors, then refinished them. I papered the walls and hung blue check curtains. My friend Dennis helped me replace two sinks and put up crisscross lattice in the yard, but I had to pay a man to install the woodstove, a large black potbelly model that I found used in the paper. I put it in the living room, next to the sofa where I presently sleep. I've given up on my bed, old lumpy thing that it is, and have gone in for sleeping in the other room, next to my books, next to my stone and leaf collections, next to an Aboriginal woodpainting Mary's aunt gave me. I sleep under my skylight, looking up at the stars. I love to think of stars like some Aborigines do, as pinholes in the heavens. I love to read, but not the books you remember me reading. I read books about the trees, about the earth, about the animals that live around me. I'm fascinated with the idea of time, that it might somehow collapse like an accordion, that it might be possible to fold it up, move it around. I like thinking that I might have many good years left, especially if time would expand like I want it to and tuck me into its grooves.

By now I have learned many things about the mountains. My friend Mary goes with me into the valley each Wednesday. We walk along the trails, asking this land for its blessing, for its force to fill me, satisfy me. It was she who taught me to make bush-devils, by rubbing a seed in my hands, how to distinguish the black ash from the scribbly gum, the mottled gum from the peppermint. She showed me where the Aborigines found ochre sand to paint themselves and where the blackbirds hid their nests. It was she who first told me the story of the Three Sisters, and I loved that image, that women could become hard and strong, fortified by the earth itself, set like sentinels to watch over the valley. I liked the idea of being visible and hidden, of being determined and unconsidered, of living outside of the boundaries of time. I asked where she'd heard that story. From her aunt, she said, who was half-Aboriginal. "I could listen to her yarn on forever," she said. It was then that I told her my daughter had once dated a half-Aboriginal man, but in the end it proved too difficult.

"It is difficult for English people to cross into the Aboriginal world," she said, "and it is difficult for Aborigines to cross into theirs."

"But why?" I asked.

"Because Aborigines were fashioned for this land, they were made from this clay." She pinched a bit of dirt from the ground and rubbed it between her fingers, then let it fall into my open hand. "Some believe that we are at the end of the age of Aborigines. Some Aborigines do not have children anymore because their children will not be true Aborigines, just as the English people will not be English people anymore. We are in a time of great transition, and after this time, no one will be the same."

"And when will this time end?" I asked.

"In a while," she said. "The English and Aborigines will be gone. Other people will come. Our grandchildren will become something else."

I picked up the ground just as she had, rubbing it between my fingers, and then she opened her hand, ready to receive my gift the way I had received hers. For the rest of the day, we walked quietly along the trails, paths that she'd learned about only as an adult. As a girl she'd been raised in a missionary school, spent time in a reform house, worked for three years as a member of a dance troupe before finally moving to the mountains. Like her aunt, she is only part Aborigine, but she doesn't know exactly how much. She is not from the Mountain Aborigines, but from Northern Queensland, where her father was once a well-known fisherman.

I don't think you'd recognize me anymore, Gregory. I'm not the young Welsh girl you once married. My skin has become thick, my fingers callused. My hair has lost its wave because on most days I wear a hat. On weekends I lead tours down into the valley, taking small groups from the Giant Stairway to Leura Falls or over to Matilda Point. I never expected people would listen to me, that I'd have ideas anyone would want to hear, but they do listen, a few even take notes. Most people are a little older, like us. They're very traditional. When I tell them about this land and the stories it holds, their faces betray a small confusion as though they had imagined it wrong, as I guess we all had. We are the lost children of the Crown, banished to the southern end of the earth. Our ancestors were shipped here, to the great prison without walls, and we will never return. We have been remade by the sun and the earth, by the blue gums arching over us.

The Three Sisters are fairly famous. Even in Melbourne, people know these pillars, the women guardians of the valley, forgotten after their father perished in that tribal war, the secret of their enchantment dying with him. What people do not know is that farther up the valley there's a smaller pillar, one standing alone, but shaped much like the Sisters, tall, segmented, sheared flat at the top. Orphan Rock, it's called, a small, overlooked monument, shadowed in this valley. I do not know its story, do not know if it even has a story, and because of this I think of it as *our* rock, yours and mine, a memorial to the life we once had, to the people we once thought we were. We are orphans, you and I, we were forgotten by the ideas that formed us. We lived during a difficult time, and I don't know when this difficult time will be over.

I wish you could see the things I see, the valley, the falls, the Sisters, how their stony peaks face the Orphan. I wish I could walk with you through this valley, that you could stand among the tourists and see how they listen to my bits of bush knowledge, how a woman in the back might write down the name of a tree or the location of a stream. Most of all, I wish you'd come with me to that small, story-less rock, that we could press our hands against it and feel how it might absorb our history, a deep murmuring inside that is in its own way inviting. I'd like to join myself with the valley, but doubt if I ever will. I'm not of the valley, but I love my life here and hope that love will offer me a small, temporary hope.

I doubt, however, that you'll ever come here. From William, I know you spend your days on the North Shore, making a living house-sitting and walking neighbours' dogs. I know your nights are spent in pubs with men like yourself, the last of the bright, sad men from England. I'd like one last chance to lie next to you, to hold you in such a way it might heal the sadness you feel. I'd like you to know me as I am now, and I'd like to know you as well. I wish you'd consider this. If I am brave I'll send this note, if not I'll keep it tucked away with the other things I've written for no one but myself. I find I tell my story over and over, and that the only one who listens is me.

Truly, with all my love,
L

* * *

The letter ends with one of the saddest images in any of her work, no one listening but her, which I think is how she must have pictured herself in her final days, alone except when she was a tour guide or when she was with Mary. I don't know if she ever sent a copy of this letter to my grandfather or if she even intended to, but I like to think she did. A few months after she wrote this letter, my grandfather died, his body unexpectedly giving out in a small twin bed, his liver swollen with undiagnosed tumors. In ways he held my grandmother to this earth. Even though they were separated, she thought of him often. Little notes marked "For Gregory" appear on many pages in her journal. Two weeks after his death, she made her famous trek into the valley, down among the rocks and trees, the fingerling streams she had named, and then she simply disappeared.

On the night I first read this letter aloud to Taylor, she looked at me, a new sadness in her eyes. Occasionally I'd read other pieces to her, ones collected into *The Bush School*, but it was this story that touched her the most, the story of my grandmother, now old, reaching out to find something she could not hold. She took off her glasses and picked up the manuscript. She held it gently in her hands, the paper brittle, semitransparent, every "t" raised a half case, which was one reason historians believe this to be one of her last written documents. In earlier manuscripts, the "t" key is not yet broken. Taylor reread the first paragraph, her lips mouthing the words, then turned to me, as if this story had explained who I was in a way she'd not understood. "Do you remember much about your grandmother?"

"I only met her that one time," I said. "I was young when she died."

"That's a shame."

"It is," I said. "I think I would've liked her."

She tucked the manuscript into its protective plastic sheath and set it on the night table, next to a glass of water and a bottle of sleeping tablets she used on a semiregular basis. When we finished talking, we turned off our lights and lay together, our hands and hips touching, my leg crossing hers at the ankle. For a while I stared at the ceiling, noticing how tiny phosphorous specks were mixed in with the acoustic molding, before I turned to her and asked, "Why did you want to know if I remembered much about my grandmother?"

"I don't know," she said. "Something in her reminds

me of you."

"We're both drawn to stories," I said. "In a way, we're both teachers."

"Aside from that," she said. "You're similar. It's very sad, I think."

"How's it sad?"

"I don't know," she said. "I just think it is." She rolled toward me, the yellow of a streetlight falling across her, illuminating her eyes, her mouth. She ran her fingers through my hair, which was something she did not do as much now that we'd been married two years. She kissed me lightly, then asked me the oddest question: "Do you think I'm pretty?"

"Yes," I said, "I think you're very pretty."

"Do you think I'm nice?"

"Yes," I said again, then I cupped my hand behind her head. "Why do you want to know?"

"Most people don't think I'm nice," she said. "I'd like you to think I am."

"You are," I said.

"I'd like you to keep thinking that because I don't know if you always will."

"Is there something I should know?" I said.

"No," she said, "nothing."

We lay there, listening to cars pass through our neighborhood, their tires spinning up our street, then slowing for the two-way stop. At times, their headlights would shine through our window, throwing shapes of light across the room, but mostly it was dark, just Taylor and me, the small space wedged between us. I listened to her breathing lengthen, felt small tremors of sleep move through her body, but before she was finally pulled under she said, "You know something?"

"No," I said, "what?"

"You should write about your grandmother."

"My grandmother," I said. "I don't think I ever could."

"You should," she said, "and I think—" The final part of that sentence I'm not sure about because she was carried off into sleep, her words hanging above us, disappearing like smoke. It was only ten minutes after eleven, relatively early for us to be in bed. I moved beside her and smoothed the hair from her face, revealing the white skin of her cheeks and forehead—skin that, when I first met her, had been tan. I began to think about what kept us together, an accountant and a school teacher, a yuppie and a loaf, but I didn't know. I knew I loved her, yet at the same time knew I was not precisely the person she wanted. She wanted someone more determined, exacting, not someone who sat back and considered things, not someone fascinated with words, with stories, with a family mostly lost.

I rested my head next to hers, the two of us sharing the same pillow, and listened to the small sounds she made in her sleep, soft faraway noises—not words, but shadow syllables, single notes caught in her throat. I should've known then that our marriage wasn't as strong as it should be, that it was like an ice statue, the warmth of each day wiping away its shape. I don't mean to say this was our last good night together— there'd be many more—but that the end was mapped across the present, tattooed on our faces, revealed in the way she placed my grandmother's manuscript on the nightstand, something inside of it scaring her away. I curled in beside her, my body warm in our nest of blankets, then put my arm around her, drawing her close. I listened to her breathing again, the rhythm always the same, two breaths, then a pause, but sleep didn't come for me. I looked at the window, the ceiling, the clock on our dresser that displayed its numbers in a red, boxy light.

At midnight I turned on my reading lamp and looked through my grandmother's manuscripts. In particular, I looked at the odd things historians decided to save: a grocery list, a recipe for pavlova, a note my grandmother had left for Mary: "M.," it read, "please tell Frank I won't be able to give tours later this week." Then she signed her name, just a flourish of indecipherable letters. I read the note four or five times, wondering if she'd written it the week she went walking off for good, an old lady of English descent making her way down the Giant Stairway one last time, but I doubt that was the note's purpose. I wondered, too, what Taylor meant when she'd said my grandmother and I were alike, but in ways I knew, though perhaps I didn't believe it at the time: we were both lost and unsure of ourselves; we were looking for love to save us in ways it would not. I kissed Taylor on the forehead once more, I looked over the note before placing it back in its protective covering, I turned off the light, then closed my eyes. Sleep would be easy for me now. The Great Dreamtime, as my grandmother called it, a place where people were at peace, where my mother was reconciled with her own mother, where my grandfather finally returned to England, a place where Taylor and I might have been one, forever holding what would be lost for us in this life.

LOVE
1980

When I was twelve I did not understand why my parents divorced, but looking back I can say with some assurance that my mother noticed other men. I do not mean she had affairs. Merely that she did not need my father as much as she once had. She had grown up in Australia and, a few years after her mother's death, found she missed her country a great deal. She wanted to see the mountains again, to hear English spoken with a Sydney accent, and to have her own stars spread out above her. She called her brother more often, spent evenings alone, and when my father realized how things might go, they planned to separate.

On May 10 my mother packed her bags and readied herself for the 10:35 flight, L.A. to Sydney direct. The last moment of tenderness I saw between my parents happened in our living room: my mother sat next to my father, her passport tucked into her pocket, her arms looped around his neck, "Still, if you ask me now," she said, "I'll rip up my ticket and stay." My father turned away sadly and when he turned back, he was close to tears. "No," he said, "it's better we do what's right." To seal this, he took her hand and kissed it. Three hours later she disappeared down a boarding ramp. The following June, I went to live with her for a year.

My mother had inherited a small mountain cottage in the township of Katoomba, not far from Sydney, a two-bedroom home, its exterior green and gold, its roof nothing more than corrugated iron. In the front yard, my uncle planted flowers and a hedge; in the back my mother strung a clothesline from the veranda to a gum tree. Each Sunday I would help her hang our laundry to dry. "There are things I do miss about the States," she said. "For one, I miss the bloody electric clothes dryers. For another, I miss pizza delivery." But she seemed, for the most part, happy there.

As for me, I liked the mountains. I liked them because they were large and open, because wallabies lived in their fields, and because gum trees covered their hills. I liked them because they held my family, and because for a while I felt special there. I was the quiet American, the one who didn't know the rules to rugby but was good in English. Most of all, I liked them because they were where I fell in love for the first time, a girl named Kelly Richardson the object of my desire.

To my surprise, my mother didn't date in Australia. At least not at first. During my childhood, she had been the type of soft, pretty, naturally flirtatious woman men often admired, but after she left my father her flirtatiousness disappeared, as did other qualities. She cut her hair; she bought darker clothes; she took an editor's job at the Historical Society. Her very mannerisms began to change, and I sensed she was slowly shifting back into the person she had been before she married.

For these reasons, I thought she would not marry again, that her time for romance had passed. She loved new things: the mountains and trees, the way a breeze could curve down from Echo Point, and how my grandmother's words sounded when she read them aloud. Each day, she rose at sunrise and sat in our breakfast nook, sipping tea and watching the fog lift out of the valley in thin, wispy clouds. Each evening, she tuned in the news, watching anchors rattle off stories about the Queen, our Prime Minister, and hostages in Iran. I thought she had found a kind of peace, brought on by her home, her work, her brother. I was surprised, then, when she started to fall in love.

At first I noticed only a change in her voice, a softness that reminded me of how she once spoke to my father. She started wearing lighter colors again— whites and pinks. In the evenings, she sat next to me, her plate in her lap, watching TV, but I could tell she was not thinking about the shows, not even *Fawlty Towers*, which was her favorite. Once, in the middle of a sitcom called *Dad's Army* she turned to me and asked, "Do you ever find it hard to be the person you're supposed to be?"

"I don't know," I said. "I guess so."

"I mean, do you ever feel a little out of sorts inside?"

"Sometimes," I said.

She got up, cleared her plate, and turned on the electric kettle, as she often did after dinner. She looked out the window, where inky hues of twilight stained the sky. When *Dad's Army* finished I set my plate beside hers. By then she had placed two teacups on the counter, in saucers patterned with delicate flowers. She put a teabag in each.

"Tell me something," she said. "Do you like it here in the mountains?"

"Yes," I said. "It's pretty nice here."

"And you don't miss being in California too much?"

"Sometimes I miss it," I said. She measured a teaspoon of sugar, carefully leveling it, and as she did, I could tell that she still pictured herself young. She was sometimes scared, as I was, but she would never tell me a thing like that. I understood, too, that she liked Mr. Richardson, though she had not yet confessed this to me.

Mr. Richardson was in his mid-thirties. Like my mother he was recently divorced, though he was still close to his ex-wife. He and my mother had met a number of times, because for the past four months I'd been dating his daughter, and on the previous Sunday, my mother had asked him to stay for afternoon tea on the back veranda. Kelly and I did not hang around long—we planned to buy magazines and read them at my uncle's nursery—but before we left I heard my mother use a line I'd only heard on TV: "You know," she said to Mr. Richardson, "I hate to have an afternoon cuppa all by myself." He turned to her, or perhaps I should say, he turned *slowly*, taking in her tone, her demeanor, the way her hands were set on her hips.

They stayed at the cottage that afternoon, Mr. Richardson in his white shirt and red suspenders, my mother wearing a pink summer dress she'd bought the previous week. When we returned, Mr. Richardson was standing on the back lawn trying to coax a wayward currawong into view by offering it bread crumbs. My mother greeted us and said, "How goes the movie page?" Kelly responded, "All the good shows come out first overseas."

From there, my mother fell in love gradually. Or at least she wanted it to appear that way. But I noticed that she walked past Mr. Richardson's store every other day, a store near the railway station called Richardson's Antiques. Both his name (Paul) and his ex-wife's name (Annette) were stenciled on the front window, though Annette no longer worked there. Local high school students had taken her place, dusting the bric-a-brac and sweeping the floor, while Mr. Richardson worked in back or stood behind the large metal cash register, his arms draped over the top of it, his fingers laced together. He was a kind, good-natured man who joked a lot: "Okay, Sam, how do you get a Kiwi to successfully manage a small business?"

"I don't know," I said. "How?"

"Flat-out simple," he replied, "you start off by giving him a large one. Get it? A large one. And he whittles it down to something small."

In the evenings, sitting in an oak chair, a banker's light behind him, he would wait for my mother as he read Tolstoy or Dickens. His eyes, magnified by reading glasses, would carefully work down each column, and then he would moisten his fingers before turning a page. When my mother arrived he looked up to find her; the doorbell jingled as she entered. He tucked his glasses into his pocket, then rose. The few times I was there, he took one of her hands and held it. I knew my mother wanted a more emotional greeting, but also knew she would satisfy herself with this elegant, somewhat formal love—which I thought would be less formal if I were not around.

"You know, Sam," he once said after my mother arrived, "it's hard to believe that a bloke like me would fall for a line like that, 'It's a shame to have a cuppa all by yourself on an afternoon like this.'"

"That's not what I said," my mother protested. "You're adding touches."

"From what I remember," I said, "it's pretty close."

"Sam, whose side are you on?" my mother teased.

"No one's."

"See?" Mr. Richardson said. "I count on Sam to be an independent observer, no real vested interest either way."

"Men always stick together," she said. "And as for you, Mister, you're lucky to get any such chatty lines, tired or not."

"Lucky?" he said. "In the antiques business, I get them all the time. You'd be surprised at the lasses that come in here on Saturdays. Real first-rate ones. You know, models and such. Once I met the girl who reads the weather on Channel Nine. She was flat-out something."

"*Lasses*," my mother repeated. "There'd better not be any lasses. I'm putting a claim on you."

"A claim," he said. "I don't know about any such claim. Seems like I just worked meself out of a different claim."

"You're the type who likes a claim and you know it."

At this he sighed. "Perhaps I do," he said, then kissed her cheek.

That night I walked out with them, Mr. Richardson locking the door behind us. Outside, the world was putting on an autumn spectacle: parkway trees had shed their leaves, the stars were beginning to dust themselves across the eastern sky, in the distance, low clouds moved along the mountains. We walked down Katoomba Street, the main thoroughfare, passing restaurants, some of them BYO, while others advertised Licensed. We walked past Lawson's Milkbar and Carraway's Fish and Chips, past touristy souvenir shops, past Mr. Rollins' camera repair. When we passed my uncle's nursery, I looked to see if he was still in the cashier's shack, but he was not. Mr. Richardson and my mother turned off on a street called Waratah, after the state flower, and continued on to Cliff Drive, where they knew a small restaurant that offered a good view of the Leura Cascades.

But I was going to see Kelly. I'd wanted to see her all day. Now that we were in Year Eight we only had one class together, and did not see each other as often as we wanted. I'd met her in November, and we'd gone on our first true date just before the Christmas holidays. We'd taken the train to Penrith, where we saw an afternoon movie, a Disney flick about two country kids who got lost in the city. Afterwards we rode the train home. The old rickety red passenger cars trudged up the mountain. Our window was open just a crack; graffiti was inked across the seat in front of us. We sat close, but I felt the space between us. I noticed the way her hands were folded in her lap, the way her shoulders were pushed slightly forward, and how her long hair had been pulled from her face and tied into a ponytail. After we'd been on the train for a while, she asked, "How come you asked me to go with you?"

"You know why," I said, "because I like you. You just want to hear me say it again."

"But how come you like me? Most boys don't. They think I'm too forceful or something."

"I don't think you're forceful."

She considered this for a moment, then asked.

"What are girls like in California?"

"Some are a lot like you," I said. Then I remembered something my dad had once said to my mom. "But not as pretty," I added.

She looked at me in a new way, her eyes a little wider, her mouth slightly open. "My father's the only one who says I'm pretty."

Though she said it truthfully, I found it hard to believe. She was the prettiest girl I'd ever met: she was tall, thin, had long, slender arms. Her hair was blonde, as were her eyebrows, her eyes blue. She had a voice I could listen to all day, and when she wanted to she could make me laugh harder than anyone I knew. On that day, though, I did not say any of these things. I simply said, "Oh."

"'Oh,'" she repeated, "you're just going to say 'oh.'"

"Oh," I said again. Then I put my hand around hers, noticing that her skin, like mine, was a little damp from the heat, from the humidity, from our nervousness. I held it for a moment, then brought it close to me, running my thumb along the curve of her index finger. We were a good ways up the mountain. The sun was low in the sky, and shadows moved through the interior of the train.

"I suppose now we're boyfriend and girlfriend," she said.

"I don't know."

"Isn't that what they do in the States? People go on a date and then they become boyfriend and girlfriend?"

"Something like that," I said. "What do they do here?"

"From what I can tell, you just go out and muck around and maybe sometime later you get married. I don't think we have rules here like you have over there."

"Which way do you prefer?" I asked.

"Oh, I don't know," she said, "American or Australian. I suppose we could try one, and if that doesn't work, we could give the other a go."

"Okay," I said, and in that moment, I started to love her. I loved her because she leaned toward me, resting her back against my chest and letting me put my arm around her. I loved her because she liked me, and I had never had a girl like me in that way before. I loved her because she felt things at a much deeper level than she let on. We rode the rest of the way like that—past Lawson, past Wentworth, past Leura. I did not say much or move, not even when my hand fell asleep, and then my arm; I was simply pleased to hold her, to be on that old passenger train on a hot December day, slowing into the station, where the stationmaster would shout "Ka-*toom*-ba" and then we'd hear doors lumbering open. I felt, for the first time, that I was occupying the space of an adult, that I was surveying the terrain and seeing how the land lay. I knew that in the future I would live within this space, but back then I could not see its importance as clearly as I see it now. On the walk home we held hands and she told me stories about her childhood, how she once lived in Melbourne, then Brisbane, and now here. "I'm like you," she said. "The whole world seems a bit strange, if you ask me."

"It seems like that to me too," I said.

For a while we fell into our own happiness: after school we would go to my uncle's nursery or visit her father. We went to the milkbar, we went to the news agent, we loitered in Mountain Books, where, when she had money, she bought thin collections of Sherlock Holmes stories. "He's just spot-on brilliant," she once told me. "I mean, I've never seen anyone as clever as he is." On Sunday afternoons we would often walk through town, sometimes to a historic house called Leurella, where she knew one of the groundsmen. Other times we explored the valley floor, hiking down the endless steps of the Giant Stairway. There, we would walk along dusty trails and sit next to streams and waterfalls, listening to the sound of a breeze moving through trees or the cries of birds. With sticks, we would write our initials in the sand, and late in the afternoon, curled next to me on a rock, she would read me a Sherlock Holmes story while the sun fell off into the horizon, projecting its color across clouds.

Once, on our way back, we found an old cave. Its interior led back only ten or twelve feet. On its walls we discovered Aboriginal handprints painted with ochre sand, dozens of them spread over gray rock like wallpaper. Toward the back, in a place where the light was dim, we saw two painted hands, separate from the others, fixed just at our height. Kelly placed her hand over one, I placed mine over the other. The rock was cold beneath our skin. After that, we sat at the entrance and kissed for a while. We were at a stage in our intimacy between kissing and making out, a place where borders were not as defined as they once had been. For the first time I felt the sadness of leaving, a sorrow stemming from the knowledge that in a few months I would board a plane and be transported back to California. I would have a different life there, a life without the mountains, without the valley, without Kelly. I believed she felt this too.

We stayed there a long time. Only when twilight began to brush its charcoal hues across the sky did we leave. We walked up the Giant Stairway—all 800-odd steps—and then continued to Martin Street, where through a window we saw our parents sitting together on the couch, her father's arm around my mother, both of them watching TV.

That night we all ate dinner together—chicken, potatoes, and green beans. We sat at the table my grandmother once owned, my mother and I on one side, Kelly and her father on the other. Mr. Richardson asked for seconds of everything. "There's nothing quite as lovely as a proper baked dinner," he said, handing my mother his plate. She seemed happy finally, and so did he. I wondered briefly if this was the type of happiness she and my father had known when they first met, but suspected it was not. My mother did not love Mr. Richardson with a youthful love, but with an older, more resigned affection. Yet during dinner she looked at him with such longing I found it difficult to watch. Kelly saw this too, then turned to me.

By mid-autumn, our lives had moved into a routine. My mother had her editing and her writing, and in the evenings she had her brother, she had me, she had Mr. Richardson. I had school, my family, and Kelly. I liked the way this granted order to my life. Each morning I woke at seven. I showered, straightened up my room, and walked out to the breakfast nook, where I often found my mother gazing out our window toward the large rock formation at the edge of the valley. When she sensed my presence, she would look at me and say, "What do you feel like—tea, crumpets, a little hot cereal?" Almost always I answered, "Just crumpets," though sometimes I had hot cereal as well. After breakfast I looked over my homework, particularly the math and history, then packed my books.

At school I endured my morning classes—English, Math, Shop—and in the afternoon I saw Kelly, first at lunch, then in History. Mr. Hansen was our teacher that term, a young, brown-haired man who only the year before had graduated from the University. He was interested in England, particularly the England of Old and Middle English, and assigned us tales about King Arthur. His favorite was *Sir Gawain and the Green Knight*. Some days he would tell us about this other England, the one poets imagined and historians half-invented. To be honest I had an easier time picturing this England than the real one that colonized Australia. The rules there seemed better defined, more straightforward: Be loyal. Treat people with respect. Do the right thing so, if for no other reason, people won't think bad of you. I knew, though, that Kelly thought these rules simplistic. One day after class she told me, "That's the problem with men," as she cleared her things off the desk.

"What do you mean, that's the problem with men?"

"Far as I can figure," she said, "men like to tie up the world with a bunch of good-sounding laws no one can live by."

"I don't think that's true," I said.

"And women," she continued, "we would rather see

things for what they are."

"I think I see things just fine," I said, but I knew in some ways she was probably right. I liked to think of the world as ordered, as just, as basically good. I believed good actions led to reward, but knew that Kelly did not see things this way.

She must have seen that she was upsetting me because she asked if I wanted to go to the milkbar. "You game for that?" she said.

"I'm game," I said, cinching my backpack closed.

When school finished, we walked to the milkbar, where we sat on bar stools. We ordered two Cokes and a basket of hot chips, which we split. We stayed there for an hour, talking to Mr. Lawson, who owned the place. Afterwards, we went to an old park bench that overlooked the valley, and as always we started in on our homework. She worked on English—*Animal Farm* was her present assignment—and I struggled with pre-algebra. When she tired of reading she moved beside me and I put my arm around her. We looked off at the valley, endless gum trees and blue sky curving down to join the earth. As we prepared to leave, she asked, "Do you reckon we'll still know each other five years from now?"

"I think so," I said. "Don't you?"

"Well," she said, "I *like* thinking that. It makes me feel good."

"Then why do you think about it any other way?"

"Who can say?" she said. "I just do sometimes."

I closed my math book, marking my place. She began to gather her things: a pencil, a highlighter, two sheets of notebook paper. By then a mist was moving down from the forest, a thin veil of dew that held the dark colors of the evening sky. I took her hand. "If you ask me," I said, "our parents get on pretty good. I think that will keep us together."

She turned to me, her thin, girlish face trying to smile, her hair no longer restrained by a band but falling free to her shoulders, and I saw that I had said the wrong thing. She moved close, and I sensed, perhaps for the first time, that she needed me to hold her. I put my arms around her, my hands clasped behind her back. "When you go back to California," she asked, "are you going to write?"

"Of course," I said.

"I mean, you'll write me just because you like me and not for any other reason?"

"I'll write you every day," I said.

"You can't write *every* day," she said. "I'd be happy if you wrote once a week."

"I will," I said. "I'll send you pictures, too."

"I'd like that," she said. "I'd like that a lot."

We began to walk home, but by then the mist had moved in around us, thick as a cloud. We were surrounded by fairy dust, by a delicate gauze, light that had become liquid and lifted itself into the air.

In the days that followed I saw how things changed between us. I don't mean they changed in large ways; the changes were small, almost imperceptible. We still met before History each day. We sat next to each other and occasionally shared a book, but in general she was not as attentive as she had been in previous classes, her book open to the wrong page, her pencil unsharpened, her eyes blankly staring at the blackboard. "The message of Camelot is simple," our teacher had written. "Man has difficulty holding on to goodness and order."

At home, too, I felt this unease, though I knew Kelly was trying to wish it away. We would sit in my backyard, near the stone birdbath, and play Checkers or read books (she with a new Sherlock Holmes and me with a book about young people on a camping trip), and sometimes during these bright autumn afternoons, she rolled over on our blanket and gave me such an honest expression of hope that my heart would almost break. On the veranda, my mother was reading my grandmother's memoirs, slowly wading through those sections she had given up on earlier. One Saturday Mr. Richardson joined us. The two of them sat in the large wicker chairs, sharing the evening paper. My mother no longer served tea; she had grown tired of that joke.

As with many things, I suppose I was the last to know. Mr. Richardson was not the man my mother had hoped. He was a good person, honest and kind, but confused about love, as I guess we all were. More specifically, he occasionally missed the company of his ex-wife. One night after my mother had cooked lasagna for him, I heard him say, "It's hard to explain." They were in the dining room; I was in my bedroom, puzzled by what my math book called "advanced variable progressions." I heard him set his silverware against his plate and then continue: "I guess what I'm getting at is, I thought things would be different." I put my book down and looked down the hallway. I saw the glow of candlelight, the stove, the sink, but could not see either of them.

I heard my mother leave her chair; its wooden legs scraped over the wood floor. I pictured her beside him, her thin hands on his shoulders, her face tilted down to see him. "Do you still get along with her?" she asked.

"In a way," he answered, "but not really."

The house began to shrink then, its sides closing in on us; we were three people under a common roof: a man, a woman, a son down the hall, his bedroom door open more than it should be. Outside, cars moved along the street; next door, the neighbors were watching *Dad's Army*; in our house, though, there was only the sound of water dripping into the sink—that and the quiet talk of my mother and Mr. Richardson.

"Do you still love her?" my mother asked, her voice almost a whisper.

"Not like that," he said. "We were married a long time. I still love her in that I want her to do well, to be happy, but not like you're thinking."

"I know how that is," she said. "I never thought

divorce could be so hard."

At that, Mr. Richardson left his chair and moved to where I could see him. He was wearing a white shirt and tie. His hands were folded together. "I shouldn't have come tonight," he said. "I'm sorry for that."

"Don't be," she said, and with a tenderness that surprised me, her arms circled his waist, her face pressed against his shoulder. He held her for a moment, the two of them close, before she said, "We're just two gay divorcés who haven't figured out what we really want." For a minute they stayed that way, their bodies swaying to imaginary music, and then he held her face with his hands, his fingers soft against her cheeks. He kissed her once, then left a few minutes later, donning his English felt hat. When he was gone I went out to see her. She stood alone, looking out our kitchen window. She was clutching a tea towel, wrapping its frayed end around her index finger and then undoing it. "Well bugger the whole world," she said, "bugger the whole bloody world."

I put my hand on her back. Her dress was damp from sweat, her ribs expanding with each breath. I didn't know what to say, or if I should say anything at all.

"Do you hate him?" I asked.

She ran her hand through my hair. "You know," she said, "I'm old enough not to hate anyone. I've done enough in my own life to teach me better." She sniffed once and then smiled, though I could tell it took effort. She lifted a dish of lasagna, offering it to me. "Care for some dinner?" she said, holding it loosely as though it were already leftovers and not something she had made only that day. "I'm going to have some more." I saw how she was trying to face this situation with bravery and grace. She was a woman with a large, sensible heart, and I admired her for that.

"Sure," I said, "I wouldn't mind some dinner. We could eat and watch TV."

"Tucker and the tube," she said, "Australiana at its best."

"We could watch the news," I said. "*Dad's Army* is already over."

"I suppose you heard," she said.

"I heard."

"Why don't you go turn on the telly? That way it's all warmed up for the news."

"All right," I said.

I continued to see Kelly after school and on Saturday afternoons. We met as we always had, though there was a desperation between us. I saw it in the way she looked at me and in the way she held my hand. When we kissed, I felt a new longing mixed with our love, a sorrow we tried to change into youthful passion. In the weeks before I left, she let me unclasp her bra and touch her breasts. Her skin was soft, and her tan lines betrayed the shape of her bathing suit—or "swimming cozzie," as she called it. We were two kids in love, fascinated with ourselves, with each other, and with the way emotion could swell inside of us.

As for my mother, she poured her efforts into work. On Sundays, though, she spent the entire day with me. The two of us would drive up to the Hydro Majestic for lunch or catch the train down to the city, where years ago she had lived in a suburb called Burwood. She did not see Mr. Richardson for a long time, but as I understand matters, sometime after I left they became friends again, meeting every few weeks for lunch or drinks. They talked about the past, their marriages long finished, and discussed how difficult the future was to grasp. "Hold on to whatever you've got, Sam," she wrote me three years before she died, "and trust it's enough to see you through."

On the Saturday before I left, Kelly and I went again to "our" cave—though now we found evidence that other people knew about it as well: cigarette stubs in the back, a beer tin stashed in a bush. We sat near the front, an old blanket beneath us. I had expected the day to be filled with great longing, but it was not. Instead we simply enjoyed being together one last time, touching, kissing, trying to remember every detail as it happened. Gradually we took off each other's shirts, leaving only our hiking shorts on, and held each other, though the previous week we had talked about doing more. As the sun moved toward the horizon, she looked at me and asked what was wrong.

"I thought it would be different today," I said. "You know, that it would feel different, because it's our last time."

She took my hand in hers, then said, "You're very emotional for a boy. It's one of the things I like about you."

"You picked a fine time to tell me," I said. "I'm

leaving next week."

She curled up beside me, her head resting on my shoulder, her arm stretched across my stomach, and a good spirit moved between us, a lightness. From the bush, we heard the sounds of currawongs, magpies, and bower birds, their songs soft, like twilight's anthem.

"You remember," I said, "on our first date, coming home on the train, you said we could try dating one way and if that didn't work out we could try the other?"

"Yes," she said.

"I was wondering which way have we been trying— the American or the Australian one?"

"I reckon the American way," she said, "otherwise I wouldn't have ended up half-naked beside some boy who's going to leave me next week."

"I don't want to go," I said. "You know that, right?"

"I know," she said. She stroked my chest and then my arms. "Tell me something," she said. "Tell me you love me."

"I love you," I said.

"And that you will always love me."

"I will," I said. "Will you?"

"Mm-huh," her voice quiet, almost a whisper.

I knew even then that these things might not prove true, though we wanted them to. We sat in a cave that, a few years later, would be closed off and protected as a historical site. The sun pulled toward the other part of the world, the part where I was from, but we did not go home. Instead we stayed down in the valley, surrounded by gum trees and mountain ash, by banksia and blackwood, by fan ferns that hung from cliffs like delicate paper ornaments. Above us blackbirds flew like shadows, across a gray sky. We stayed there well past seven o'clock, the evening chill making us feel oddly alive, until moonlight spilled like milk down around us.

Later, as we walked up the Giant Stairway for the last time, she said, "You're really going to write me?"

"Every week."

"I thought it was every day."

"It was," I said, "but you said that was too much."

"Oh, I reckon every day might not be too much, at least at first."

"I'm a fair writer," I said.

"I'm not so good, but I'll give it a go."

That was all we said about it, perhaps because we knew how things would turn out. We'd write for a while, our letters filled with longing, but eventually our emotions would be less intense, the letters less frequent, just a few a year—at Christmas or on birthdays—until those stopped as well.

On that night, though, we simply took each other's hands and walked back to my mother's house, where lights illuminated the front windows, and where a woodstove filled the rooms with its heat. There we would talk, have tea, and finally kiss more after my mother went to bed. At eleven-thirty Kelly's father arrived to pick her up. He did not come to the door or honk, but simply flashed his highbeams toward the front windows. I walked her to the car, said hello to her father, then watched them drive away. The car grew smaller and smaller, its brake lights dimmer and dimmer, until its shape was finally indistinguishable from all the other things I remember about living in that quiet mountain town.

THE WOMAN OF STONE
1996–1998

This final story is not so much about my family as it is about me.

I'm an English teacher. I work at a moderate-sized public high school in a small coastal town north of Los Angeles. I came into teaching because, as a college student, I'd been somewhat lost. Unable to tell my own story, I clung to stories I read in books and saw on film. In my junior year, I fell in love with a girl named Taylor, a finance major who, looking back, I can say was more directed and confident than I was. She knew how to avoid questions without answers, which was one of the reasons I loved her. She came from a strong, traditional family—her father a dentist, her mother a homemaker—while I came from a family broken in many ways. As a teenager I'd learned how to accommodate grief and absorb it, and consequently I did not learn how to express myself in ways that would have satisfied Taylor and made our marriage more secure. Instead, like many people I knew, I stumbled into teaching, a profession I've come to enjoy and respect.

Unlike most English teachers, I had no early delusions about being an author—many of my colleagues have a half-finished novel tucked away in a drawer—but I was quite content reading and discussing the books I assigned each year. I taught a variety of courses, but more often than not, I taught eleventh- and twelfth-grade literature, which meant each August I would select eight novels for the coming semester (Faulkner, Fitzgerald, Melville, Wharton, Morrison, and so on) and plan essay assignments around each one. In my third year of teaching, however, our state-mandated curriculum changed so that, even though I taught literature, I was also required to assign one personal essay that students were to write in response to the reading. Just how an eleventh-grader was supposed to write a personal essay in response to *Moby Dick*, I wasn't sure, but I went ahead and assigned these essays. After a while I found I was good at teaching the personal essay. Some of my students' essays reached fifteen pages. Occasionally I'd receive an essay that broke through the twenty-page mark. And it wasn't just the number of pages that impressed me. I was impressed by how thoughtful my students could be while under the influence of a book.

The fall I was thirty I thought I'd try to write an essay along with my class. I knew that my youth and the years of my first marriage would soon fade, slipping into a less tangible memory if I didn't find some way to preserve them. Earlier that year I'd moved in with Jolene, a wonderful woman who taught art history at our school. In class, as an exercise, I asked my students to come up with a list of images they might use in their essays—vivid, revealing images that had some emotion behind them. As they did this, I sat at my desk and began a list for my own story: "Frost. Trees. Cliffs like polished steel." It was this last image that held me because for a moment it made me feel what it was like to live in Australia all those years ago.

At first I wanted to write about my entire life in one essay—my childhood, my mother, my father, my grandmother and grandfather—but found I couldn't pack it into such a small space. For an English teacher, I had very little idea of how a story was constructed, what could be included and what couldn't, and for the first time I felt a certain respect for my fellow teachers who'd been working on their own writing projects all these years. Over time I saw that my first story would be about my grandmother's influence on our family. I wanted to present my grandmother as I understood her, mainly from conversations with my mother—as a woman who stood apart from the rest of her generation. She divorced her husband, lived alone, and eventually disappeared on a bushwalk. For months I'd been thinking of her, how her story had been scripted for Australian radio and how it was being developed into a stage play, but these versions lacked something essential. They portrayed her as a single-minded heroine without acknowledging her tragic, human legacy, namely that of the people who survived her. In the past few months, I'd felt her presence in a way I have trouble describing—a lingering sensation, an awareness of memory—and when Jolene and I went through my grandmother's old journals I was drawn to them in a new way. I found a yearning in her writing, a hopefulness, a determined innocence, as if she didn't know how her actions would affect others, particularly my mother, who, for most of her life, longed for maternal attention.

I worked with this essay a little each day, staying as close to family truth as I could. By the time my own students turned in their final drafts, I only had seven or eight different beginnings, no body, no structure, and certainly no closure. I read through my students' essays with an admiration I hadn't had in previous years. I don't mean to say I admired all of them—Ken Scofield, for example, produced a poorly written account of his first date, and Candace Leigh turned in a paper she'd written the year before—but many were quite good. Or so I thought in light of my own inability to write. Only after the term was over and I had the time to really study my grandmother's journals was I able to see part of the story I'd always sensed was in my family. Surprisingly I found this story difficult to tell because I was in it and had been affected by it—the story of how my grandmother and mother came to their ends, the same bushwalk, the same trail, the same time of year.

I divided the essay into small sections (one on my

grandfather, one on my grandmother, one on my mother growing up) and found that if I changed my name—that is, if I called myself Sam Browne—I could write about my own experience with more objectivity. I could see myself from outside my body which was something I hadn't been able to do until now. All through Christmas break, I worked on my essay, rearranging the sections, playing with the sentences. I feared I might be pushing Jolene away, as I was often distracted or moody, yet I couldn't stop writing. Jolene and I had been living together for six months, and I knew there was still a tentativeness to our love, a hesitation that I attributed to both of us remembering the sting of divorce. On December 27, while she was exchanging a few Christmas gifts, I stayed in my room for thirteen hours. I was not really writing so much as I was carefully reading my grandmother's journals, sounding out old words. Only twice did I stop—once to make toast and once to check the mail, hopeful that a set of research papers might have arrived from my uncle.

The week before I'd asked him to send a few newspaper articles published just after my grandmother's death, one of which was accompanied by photographs. "That old rubbish," he'd said. "What on earth do you want with it?"

"I'm writing something," I said.

"Well now, you are your mother's son, aren't you?"

"I guess I am," I said.

Somewhere around that time Jolene took an interest in my project. She had once been an artist, and though we often read to each other in bed, she was more affected by images than by words. At night, instead of reading *The New Yorker* or an essay by Updike or Hughes, she opted for something my grandmother had written, often asking me to read individual sentences more than once, her eyes rolling toward the ceiling as though she were weighing its truth. Her favorite line was one of description: "Each evening, I sit on my veranda and wait for the kookaburras to roost in my gum tree, their laugh a sadly comic greeting." Even now I cannot explain her connection to this line—the sadness perhaps or the image of solitude—but she saw something in this sentence that explained my grandmother in a way the other sentences did not.

For a while I began to wonder about her interest in these journals. I wondered if she was able to understand them in a way I couldn't. I wondered if an honest examination of my grandmother's story might damage me as it had my mother. Carefully I worked to assemble this story, and when I had a full draft, I offered it to Jolene. She read it the next day, and from the way the pages were crinkled I knew she'd read it more than once. More importantly, she left me notes about the ending. At the end of the essay, I stand atop a cliff looking into the valley, toward the trail my grandmother and later my own mother followed. My grandmother's body, I explain, was never found, but fifteen years later, my mother's was, curled by a small pool.

That night after dinner, we talked about my essay, which by now I was calling "The Australia Stories." I knew she liked it but was troubled by it as well. "The conclusion," she said, "where you look into the valley, it doesn't feel right. Something's missing."

"I was hoping you wouldn't notice that. I feel it, too, but I don't know what to put there. I mean, I don't know how to end it. It's as though it doesn't have a true ending and I need to manufacture one."

"Well," she said, "what did you feel when you stood there?"

"I was thinking about my mother," I said. "I was missing her. I was also thinking about my grandmother."

"What about your grandmother?"

"How she was so strong-willed and determined. I was wondering what my mother would've been like if my grandmother had been different."

"I like that she was strong-willed."

"I do, too," I said, "but still I wonder."

Later that night in bed, we leafed through my grandmother's journals. I had the originals, all except for a few I'd given to a national museum in Canberra, Australia. Together, we read from the pages she'd written the year before she died, notes to herself, some chapters for a book she was never able to publish, a letter to my mother that began, "If I could give you one gift, I would give you freedom, all the freedom in the world, freedom to live as you wanted, without regard for anyone." Oddly this was the one gift my mother didn't want. She didn't want freedom, but to tie herself as closely to her family as she could.

Again, I felt a certain wonder that I was holding the paper my grandmother had held thirty or forty years before. I was writing about a ghost, someone who existed for me only in spirit, a woman I'd met just once when I was very young, though every year or two I'd get a letter from an English or Australian reporter who wanted to know details about her, stories I couldn't possibly have known unless my mother or my uncle had told me.

That night I went to bed frustrated, thinking about the end of my essay, the section where I appear for the first time, a young college student visiting his uncle in Australia. On a Thursday afternoon, I travel by commuter train to the Blue Mountains. I walk to my grandmother's cottage and then to the cliffs. As a teenager I explored the valley and took Kelly there. But I don't think about these things. I think only about my mother and grandmother—how much that valley has taken from me.

I stayed awake until two. In my mind I began to take apart my essay and examine each piece: the section about my grandmother, the section about my grandfather, and the one about my mother. After considering them, I wondered how I could rewrite the final page. I felt I'd taken the right road to the wrong end. As I went to sleep, I was still picturing myself at the cliffs, the valley beneath me, but sometime later I was carried through the valley. Gum trees thick around me, ferns carpeting the earth. I was quiet. I listened for things, but heard little. No birds. No people. Just a breeze fluting through the leaves.

When I woke, I didn't feel rested. I knew this was somehow caused by the strangeness and realism of my dream. Jolene was lying beside me, her eyes open, her head pillowed by an arm. "You know something, sweetheart," she said. "You snore."

"Just tell me to roll over. That usually works."

"I did. You just lay there."

"Well then," I said and kissed her, "you should've given me a little push."

A few minutes later, I got up, and while Jolene was taking her shower, I toasted bagels and made coffee. I thought about my dream, how I had not stayed at the top of the valley, as I had in my essay, but instead ventured into it. I remembered the soft breeze, the silence. I wanted to stay there, down where it was quiet, a feeling of solitude rising in me. When Jolene joined me, dressed for work, she said, "It's very odd. I lose sleep and you look tired."

"Do I really look tired?"

"Yes," she said, "you do."

"I had strange dreams."

She began to spread cream cheese over her bagel. "You look like grad students I used to know."

"Which ones?"

"The ones who painted too much."

"I was afraid you'd say that."

She touched my hand gently as if she understood me in a way I could not understand myself. "You don't need to torture yourself. The essay will come in its own time. Waiting is the hardest part."

"That's difficult advice to follow." I walked to the kitchen, where I poured more coffee into my cup. She sat at our table in jeans and a fitted wool jacket. I thought about how much I loved her and, at the same time, how difficult it could be to hold on to love. "Tell me again," I said, "why you stopped painting."

"I like teaching better. I like being with people." She

took a bite from her bagel, then set it back on her plate. "You know," she said, "real-world concerns."

In the days that followed I tried not to think about my essay. I put it aside like a difficult decision I wasn't ready to make. Even when the package from my uncle arrived, I looked through it only once, lingering on photos of my mother and grandmother, how beautiful they had been, how serious, and then set them beside my grandmother's journals. I began to look at my essay with a more critical eye. I could see myself as Sam Browne, a person who was not quite me, a younger man having experiences almost identical to my own. It was a mental trick, but effective. Looking at my writing from this perspective, I could see elements of tragedy turning inside my family. I understood the desperation that pulled my grandparents apart and that later caused my mother to return to Australia. Then I wondered if such compulsions were inside of me. My grandmother had tried to spin her life out as a story, and later this story captivated my mother to the point where little else mattered. I knew, too, that stories affected me in ways they did not always affect other people. I was amazed when a book like The Catcher in the Rye or even The Great Gatsby didn't produce the same dreaminess in my students that it produced in me. Often it was the quiet ones, usually a few of the girls, who were touched by this dreaminess. I recognized the sheen in their eyes, the way they sat on benches at lunch rereading their books instead of talking to friends.

In college, a professor once told me that we tell ourselves the stories we need to be told, and I wondered why I needed to be told *all* the stories over and over, book after book. I taught them as much for my students as I did for myself. The term after I started writing about my family, I was amazed each novel had an ending, and that each ending functioned much like a door, either opening or closing for the main characters. My problem was simple: I couldn't find such a door in my own story. My family's experience was a wide-open room, no walls, no windows in sight.

When I tired of considering the essay alone, I asked some of my fellow teachers to read it, and when they brought it back I asked about the ending. Even Tony Rodriguez, who'd actually published a book of stories, thought it worked fairly well. I believed my colleagues were honest with me. If they had disliked the ending, they would've told me. But still I wondered why both Jolene and I focused on this one element, picturing my essay like an orchestra that, just before the end of a performance, momentarily alights on the wrong chord before correcting itself.

Every time I looked at the essay, I felt the strangeness in its closing scene. I tinkered with it, believing the true ending was somewhere inside me. Because I understood its falseness, I reasoned, I should also understand how to fix it. Each Saturday, I'd read my essay aloud, and in a way I find self-indulgent to admit, I enjoyed the sound of my own words. When I'd written these sentences I'd occupied a part of my mind much more perceptive than the part I usually occupy. I'd sensed a direction in my family which now, months later, I still did not understand.

A few times, after picturing the valley, I attempted to sketch it, working the long lines of cliffs across typing paper—the trees, the stairway, the Three Sisters. By the end of the month, I had five such drawings to help me visualize how my grandmother saw her world, the trees lush against the hillside, the valley opening up to a deep floor, wind-carved rocks rising like withered people. I looked at these pictures, which I kept in my desk drawer, trying to inhabit my grandmother's world, to view it as she must have. But as I looked at them I became more convinced my grandmother was outside my grasp, that she lived in a country I no longer understood. I'd visited Australia many times, had in fact lived there, but the place rested in my past, like that far-off garden that, according to some religions, humanity left so many years ago. At last I decided that these were my pictures, impressions of my memories, and hardly tied to my grandmother at all, though I wanted them to be. The valley she saw was different from the one I remembered. By now I was thirty-one years old and had trouble walking back in time and becoming the person who, in my essay, I called Sam Browne, a younger man who seemed to have a fair understanding of life that over the years I had somehow lost.

As the term progressed, I wrote more about this person, Sam Browne. As I did, I found I liked him, which surprised me. Growing up, I didn't know if I'd like myself, but as I looked at him now in writing, I did in fact like him. I believed his first girlfriend, Kelly, would've liked him, as would his wife, Taylor, though he was probably not well suited for either of them. In ways, he was lost, but his displacement was different from the usual variety I saw around me: he held on to many things, his uncle, his teaching, his idea of love, which was bigger than perhaps it should've been. By that, I mean his idea of love had been influenced by a family that was difficult to know—a family that occasionally hid its emotions behind grand achievements. This might be why I love stories so much, why they rouse me, why they produce a coppery yearning in my chest. I understand them in ways I cannot understand my own family. I was writing these stories not so much for other people but for myself. I hoped to teach myself something, but the only lesson I'd learned so far was partially concealed in the ending of the first essay, musical notes knotted into the wrong chord. But somehow those same notes might also be reworked into the chord that should be there, a fuller, more accurate sound.

Over the following months, I began to work on other essays about my childhood and my time in Australia, but still that first essay haunted me. I believed my family's story did not end there, with me looking into the valley, but somewhere else, a vista I couldn't yet see. Within the logic of the story, everything should be over—my grandmother had died, as had my mother—but yet I understood it wasn't over. There was some turn I had missed.

By the time summer school was half over, I'd finished three essays and was beginning a fourth—one about how my marriage ended, though even this one, I knew, was tied to Australia. I'd tried writing about other aspects of my life—such as my father and my life in America—but each time, I felt the tension leave my words: they were as lifeless as lint. I began to see my essays as questions I couldn't answer. These questions were tied to the great southern continent. I belonged to it, yet I didn't belong because I hadn't grown up there. Still I felt its presence, like breath, but as I grew older it began to diminish, moving away like a previous life I no longer could claim as my own.

At about this time, Jolene found my drawings of the

Blue Mountains. Though I didn't hide them, I was surprised when I saw her looking at them. Her eyes were wide and focused, and as I sat next to her, she didn't look at me, but continued to examine my work. She was looking at one I'd sketched roughly from Echo Point, a combination of memory and photos, nothing more than outlines made in pencil and a few smudge marks. I explained I'd done them months ago, when I was still thinking about my first essay.

"These aren't bad," she said, tilting the paper so I could see it. "It has a curious perspective. You said you made them from memory, right?"

"And from photos."

"Well, for some reason, you've chosen to draw each of them from above, as though you are fifty feet tall or something."

"I hadn't really noticed that," I said, but I saw what she meant: in my drawings, I was forever looking down at the world. I had fixed myself above the earth, like a low cloud.

"It takes forever for my students to do this."

"To do what?"

"To play with perspective like that. To detach

themselves. In each of their paintings, the perspective is normal, fixed. It shows nothing new."

"To be honest, I wasn't trying to do anything at all. I was only trying to remember things."

For the rest of the day, on and off, I wondered about this, why I'd visualized the Blue Mountains this way. I'd lived there, gone to school there, I'd stood at Echo Point, my fingers curved around the metal rail on mornings so cold mist poured down cliffs like cream. Still I could not view the land as a person who'd lived there. Instead I hovered overhead, searching for something, but what? To rescue my mother? To save the young Sam Browne who, over time, would grow up and become me? Then I noticed something else: I hadn't placed any people in my drawings, and for some reason this puzzled me. Why would I leave the valley so empty?

Later that night, Jolene and I ate dinner by the beach. We walked along the shore and talked about summer school classes we were teaching and about marriage, which was something we rarely talked about. We were in love, but we'd been in love with other people before. I wanted the impossible, to know that our love wouldn't fall apart like the love I'd shared with Taylor. At home, we tumbled into bed a little drunk. We made love, but it was different that night. There was a warm strangeness between us, a desperation in our movements, in the way our hips arched together and the way she circled her fingers around my wrists to keep my hands close to her chest. I kissed the soft skin of her neck. I ran my hands down the length of her arms. With my finger I traced her eyebrows and then the beautiful lines that graced the corners of her mouth. Afterward, I lay beside her, her head cradled in my arms, and for the first time in my life, I repeated the phrase *I love you* until my voice wore thin. All other words had disappeared, leaving only these three, as if they could form their own complete language. At the time, I thought our drinking had helped open this rare place—I'd had three beers and a gin and tonic—but looking back I don't believe that to be true. Four drinks is not a lot for a man my size.

As far as I know we fell asleep beside each other, and as I was pulled under, I was aware of a great darkness, no sky, no earth, no water, just the nothingness that existed before time, then slowly light penetrated this world, revealing trees and rock, a sky so blue I could weep. I was in the Blue Mountains, looking at the Jamison Valley. As in my drawings, I saw the landscape from above, fixed like a bird in a tree, and knew, too, that this dream was much stronger and clearer than the dream I'd had months before. I saw people finally enter the valley, dozens of them, but they weren't the people I recognized from my trips to Australia. They wore T-shirts and jeans. They drove Holdens and late-model imports. They gathered at Echo Point and looked at the Three Sisters. A man selling hot dogs set his pushcart beside a small grassy area. Then I heard a soft, thin voice, which had probably been there the whole time, though I hadn't noticed it. "Stone," it whispered, "I am stone." I listened, mesmerized, and then, as though my dream had reached its apex and had begun to retrace its steps, I stopped hearing the voice. Gradually darkness began to shroud my vision, until I couldn't see the valley at all.

I woke well before sunrise, the moonlight almost tangible in our room, and turned toward Jolene, who was still asleep. She lay there, head centered on the pillow, hands folded over her chest. As I watched, small tremors moved through her body, tiny quakes along her fingers and legs, nothing more than is normal to sleep, but that night I was fascinated by it, how her body moved under unconscious power. I smoothed the hair from her face, then settled beside her and tried to sleep myself. But true sleep didn't come, only a kind of half sleep I remembered from my college days, a wishful anxiety I couldn't push away.

In the morning, Jolene didn't get up right away, but stayed in bed, her body curled toward mine, her fingers absently brushing the hair on my arm. I knew something had changed between us and that this feeling was something good, but at the same time didn't yet trust it. I believed she sensed it too, this change.

Before getting up, she turned to me, hesitation in her eyes, and asked, "What did your grandmother's voice sound like?"

I looked at her. "I dreamt about the valley, too."

"Odd," she said, "isn't it?"

"Yes."

"Schoolteachers in summer, not enough for us to think about."

She kissed me, then I felt part of our tenderness leave as she made her way toward the shower.

For the rest of the week, we were conscious of the closeness that had opened between us. She told me things about her childhood I hadn't known, and I told her about my life in Australia. At the same time, however, I knew this closeness could not be relied on. It might close up, vanish, returning us to the two people we'd been the previous week, good-natured individuals who did in fact love each other, though their love was a common love and maybe not strong enough to carry them through to the end of their lives. It was the type of love I'd once felt for Taylor and, I thought, the type of love Jolene might have felt for her ex-husband as well. Without realizing what had happened, we had slipped into an unusual and unreliable realm.

Jolene didn't forget that dream—the one we seemed to share—and looking back, I understand our dreams might have been entirely separate, inspired by the pictures I'd drawn. More than once that week she looked at my drawings, trying to figure out their balance and scope, studying the gray shadows in the background, an elusive depth I'd rubbed into the paper while my third-period juniors were working on an in-class writing exercise. At school, she struggled to be the person she had been, the quiet, warm art teacher who, during her second year in grad school, had given up on a painting career. Several afternoons I'd found her alone in her classroom, staring at an art slide she'd used earlier that day, its image projected on a reflective white screen. Once, when I entered her classroom, she was looking at a painting from Picasso's blue period. A coffin was centered at the bottom of the canvas, but up above, harlot angels greeted the departed man's ghost. "You know what I like about this?" she said.

"No," I said, "what?"

"I like that there's more passion in this painting than one would think the colors could possibly produce. I haven't thought about paintings like this for a long time, and it scares me."

"Scares you? Why?"

"I don't know, but it does."

For the next few days Jolene stayed after school looking at art slides, her hands neatly folded in her lap, while on her desk, in a mug a student had given her, her tea grew cold. Four or five afternoons I arrived at her classroom, a pile of student essays bundled under my arm, only to find her sitting there, oblivious to my presence. In truth, I loved watching her like that—how serious she appeared, how her trained eyes worked over every inch of an image, studying it for meaning and technique. Usually I stood quietly at her door. I was glimpsing a part of her I didn't fully know. I loved that I didn't know her as completely as I felt I'd known Taylor. Even if I were to be with Jolene for the rest of my life, as I hoped, I wouldn't be able to riddle through all of her complexities. In certain ways, she'd exist apart from me. We'd have our own space together, yet she'd have a private space as well. For some reason, I needed that.

"What are you doing?" I asked one afternoon as I walked into her classroom.

"I'm thinking," she said. "A student asked me a question about Cubism. He wanted to know if the twentieth century was the century when everything fell apart. I knew what he meant, was this the century when we destroyed how we'd come to see the world? I was going to tell him yes, but then I wasn't sure if I believed that or not. I think I do, but can't really say."

I sat in one of the student chairs next to her. I took her hand and held it. It was warmer than I'd expected. "Are you going to start painting again?" I asked.

"No. Not for a long time, if ever."

I smoothed my thumb over her fingers. "Are you worried about us?"

"No," she said. Only then did she look at me, the man who, over a year ago now, had fallen in love with her.

She hesitated, glancing down at her desk, then back at me.

"Then what?" I asked.

She walked to her desk, running her hands down the front of her shirt. "You'll think I'm crazy if I tell you."

"I won't think you're crazy," I said.

"You will," she said. She sat on her teachers' desk, a large smooth surface that, unlike mine, was not cluttered with student essays and old attendance rosters. "But I'll tell you anyway." I waited for her to begin, and as I did an anxiousness entered me. She looked at the large acoustic panels that covered her ceiling. "Those pictures you drew, I dream about them sometimes. You know, I see them when I'm dreaming. The trees. The rocks. The entire valley. I see them the same way you drew them, from above. But these dreams, they aren't like other dreams. They're more vivid, more exact. What I mean is, they feel real to me. I can't explain why."

"I had that dream about the valley, too," I said. "I told you that."

"I've had it more than once," she said, "and each time, I hear a voice, a small, lilting voice I think is the voice in your grandmother's journals. I know, we've read those journals many times. I thought this was nothing more than passing fancy, but I can't shake the feeling."

"I heard a voice in my dream, too," I said.

"It's not a voice really, but something odd. It repeats itself. It speaks in short sentences. Even dreaming, I somehow think I'm tricking myself into hearing it. I'm very conscious in these dreams. I mean, I know I'm dreaming."

"In my dream, she said she was stone."

"She told me she was content and sad. She said she saw your mother walk into the valley. She said your mother spoke to her by the water." Jolene smoothed stray hairs behind her ears and then folded her hands into her lap. She was breathing deeply. "I know all these things from reading about her. The funny part is I'm afraid because I've fallen in love with you, and I hadn't meant to fall in love like this. I hadn't meant to need anyone this way. This is why I'm dreaming these dreams. I'm dreaming crazy dreams because I'm afraid."

"That's not why," I said.

"You're a romantic. You think life should hold more than it does. I like that about you. I've always liked romantics. I'm a person who surrounds herself with romantics because she can't be one herself."

"Would you tell me something," I said, "if I asked?"

"Of course," she said, "anything."

"Did you ever love your ex like this? I mean, did you ever feel this way?"

Her eyes narrowed. "No," she said, "I never meant to slip in this deep, not with anyone."

For the rest of the day I tried to re-create our old

comfortable life. I sliced up brie and set it on a small platter with a plate of crackers. I opened a bottle of white wine and brought it outside where I found her grading freshman quizzes. I sat beside her and, as was our routine months ago, I graded papers, but I couldn't keep my mind on my work, not even when one student, Shirley Myers, wrestled with the existential questions that plagued Melville. After tallying up grade points, Jolene turned to me, holding a quiz, and said, "It's amazing that some students can remember all the paintings, in detail even, and still not be affected by them."

"Paintings?" I said. "You should see what they do to books."

At this she laughed, which for a moment made me feel relieved, as though she were no longer afraid, but I knew, despite this, that she still was.

Later that evening, I took a book by our old standby, John Updike, from the shelf and picked out a story to read to her—a short, happy tale about people somewhat like us, divorced and drawn to love again. We watched the moon rise through our window, waxing toward fullness, and once we'd finished the last of the wine, we lay next to each other in bed. She was wearing a cut-off T-shirt and a pair of my old boxer shorts, while I was wearing nothing more than thin pajama bottoms because the nights had turned warm. I felt desire growing between us and knew, at the same time, that she was trying to hold it at a distance where it was more controllable and safe. Instead of kissing her, I traced a line down her body, over the bridge of her nose, across her lips and along the delicate hollow of her throat, between her breasts and into the shallow incline of her stomach. Again I saw that her breathing was faster than usual. "If I see you dreaming, do you want me to wake you?" I asked.

She stiffened. "No," she said. "I want to see what's there. I mean, now that I've built it up, it will probably all go away, won't it?"

"I watched you once," I said, "while you were dreaming. Your fingers moved a little, like you were trying to touch something."

"Maybe I was," she said, then she moved closer to me. "I like that you know that about me. It's something I could never know about myself."

"Your fingers move and sometimes you open your

lips, but you never say anything."

"Mmm," she said and closed her eyes, bringing the thin percale sheet to her shoulders. "Tell me something," she said, "do you think you'll always love me?"

"That's what I want to happen."

"Do you think it will?"

"Yes," I said. "And what about you, is that what you want to happen?"

"I do, but sometimes it frightens me."

I ran my fingers through her hair, and she started to fall asleep. Her breathing lengthened, and a stillness began to claim her. I looked for that great darkness, the one I'd glimpsed only once, but it wouldn't come. Neither would sleep. Over the past few weeks she'd come to own me in a way I'd never been owned before, and I liked that, having someone to belong to, a place that was home, and I wanted to hold on to these feelings forever. When I knew I wouldn't sleep, I left her, the sheet tight around her shoulders, her hands clasped under her chin.

I went to the den to read more student essays, but I couldn't focus on them, not even on the ones written by my favorite students. I thought I might write, but knew that would be futile as well. Instead, I stared out the window. I looked at cars, how their headlights moved down the street, two dimes of light. I was about to go to bed when I saw the box containing my grandmother's journals. I had not looked at them in weeks, but in that moment, I felt drawn to them. I removed a folder and looked through the pages, the odd assortment of leftover manuscripts, letters and grocery lists, all collected by my mother as if, by the sheer accumulation of words, she might find her mother's affection bundled in with the paper and ink.

I read a note my grandmother had left for her best friend, Mary, "I think I might raise some chooks in back, have proper omelets every Sunday. What do you think?" Then I looked at some of the things she'd once tried to publish. I was struck by their serious tone, how in places she catalogued elements of the small town she'd once lived in: the bottle shops, the milkbars, the outdoor movie theaters where the audience sat on wooden bleachers, the traveling boxing shows that featured men who fought inside canvas tents her uncle had helped erect. I held on to these images for a while and then thought about her life, how she'd been born in a small town, later moved to Sydney, and then turned her back on all the modern city had to offer and returned to the mountains. In her last years, she even turned her back on that and decided to find a place for herself in the bush, first as a hiker and later as a guide, trying to understand her world as it might have been before the Europeans arrived. In the back of the box, mixed in with the things my uncle had recently sent, I found a picture of my grandmother as a girl of about ten or twelve. She wore a dark dress, her hair pinned into a bun. She looked wearily at the camera as though she already knew the arc of her life, how difficulties would shape her into a woman strong enough and hard enough to live alone in the mountains. I put back the picture but kept thinking about what it revealed— her innocence, her determination, her yearnings, an odd combination both of her children inherited in one way or another.

I returned to our bedroom but didn't open the door right away because I began to sense a presence in our house, one which I'd never felt before, a thickness in the air that somehow altered the emotional balance to which I'd grown accustomed. Jolene was in bed, the thin sheet tucked around her, her breathing slow and steady, but as I walked toward her, I noticed small movements through her fingers, the momentary contraction of individual muscles, then their release. I knelt beside her. I considered waking her, but remembered she'd asked me not to. Instead, I remained beside her, noticing small movements in her fingers, the gentle turn of her knee. When she opened her mouth, I leaned forward, listening for what she might say. Only air escaped from her lips, a sweet rhythmic breathing that had often lulled me to sleep, but in one of these breaths I heard the hint of a word, a syllable. I put my hand near hers, and sensing this, she moved hers toward mine. Then in a whisper, I said, "Where are you?"

Even though her eyes were closed, she furrowed her brow in concentration. "A valley." She worked her fingers, as if counting invisible beads.

"Are you in danger?"

"No," she said.

I moved closer. Her fingers slowed, but her knees shifted again. She lay in the moonlight, the windows closed, though a slow, almost imperceptible breeze moved between us.

"Are you alone?" I asked.

"No."

"Then who's with you?"

"A woman," she said.

"Who is the woman?"

"A woman," she repeated.

"Is she there now?"

"No."

"Where is she?"

"She's not from here."

"Where is she now?"

Again confusion began to move across her face, her eyebrows slanting together. "She could not stay," she said.

"But she's with you now?"

"Yes," she said.

"And she's in the valley?"

"She was here," she said.

"Where is she?"

"She was here," she said again, her voice growing thin, sliding away into breath. Her fingers began to finish their movements, touching the air as if she were touching individual keys on a piano, then she curled into the position she assumed when she fell asleep, her legs tucked slightly toward her stomach, her hands clasped beneath her chin.

"Where are you now?" I asked, but she didn't answer. She closed her lips, her mouth momentarily twitching, then drawing still again. "Are you in the valley?" I asked, but again my question was met with silence. She lay there, her face pale with moonlight. I touched her forehead, testing for a fever, but she was as cool as a cucumber. Standing there, my hand on her shoulder, I felt the presence begin to leave our house, the air thinning. The room became cold. I walked to the hallway. I saw our porch light flicker off for a moment, then turn on again.

By then, it was after two o'clock. I was more tired than I'd been in weeks. Finally I went to bed, lying beside Jolene who, I suspected, was holding on to a dream she'd remember for the rest of her life, the type of dream people rarely have. I fell asleep slowly, aware of the noises around us—the cars, a breeze, even my neighbor's tap dripping into a sink. In that twilight realm between consciousness and full sleep, when I still had some control of my mind, I expected a dream to overtake me, to see colors I could not name, but such a dream didn't come, nor did the unfathomable darkness I'd experienced months ago. Instead I was carried off into my usual variety of worried sleep. I did in fact dream, but it was not one of those vivid, otherworldly dreams, just a regular dream. For a while I was twenty-eight again. I was leaving Taylor. In the dream my departure felt unquestionably right; whereas in life I hadn't felt that way at all.

The next morning, when we awoke, I saw that Jolene was rested, her eyes bright, her face slightly blushed. I expected her to be nervous, frightened even, but she wasn't. I put my hand on her knee, then asked about the dream. "I thought maybe we could just lie here for a moment before we talked," she said. She ran her fingers across my face, and in response, I put my arm around her. Her body was very relaxed, and I knew somehow this had been brought about by her dream. I kissed her lightly, and she kissed me back.

Over breakfast she told me about her dream, how again she'd floated over the valley, the earth beneath her, the sky an endless blue. "I wanted to go down into the valley, to walk," she said, "but somehow I knew that I couldn't. This was all there was. I was tied to this other consciousness up here. It was very peaceful, and I could feel that peace fading away. It was odd, how deeply I felt everything." She ate a piece of the bagel I'd toasted for her, then set it on her plate. Only then did she look at me, a question evident in her every feature. "Do you think I'm crazy?" she asked.

"No," I said, "not at all."

"It's not a matter of believing," she said, "but of—of something else. I'm not sure what. Accepting. Or just letting it affect you. I don't know."

I offered her more orange juice. "Do you remember me asking you questions last night, when you were dreaming?"

"How did you know I was dreaming?"

"Your fingers," I said, "they were moving."

She touched her fingers, remembering. "What did you ask?"

I told her what I'd asked and how she'd responded. She was in a valley, a presence with her. As I described that conversation, her face took on an expression of gentle acceptance, as if she didn't remember her answers but they all made a certain sense to her and had the feeling of truth. "I could've said those things," she said at last, "but I don't remember talking. I do remember that time had an odd feel up there, like days could go on forever. But I'm not sure why I know that either."

Twice during our drive to school, I turned to find her looking at me, a softness in her eyes. We taught our classes, and after school I went to her classroom, where again I saw her looking at slides projected onto the reflective screen, her arms crossed, an air of concentration about her as if she were still trying to understand the elusive language of the images. I noticed that her concentration was not as deep as it had been on previous days. Part of her obsession was falling away, leaving the person I knew, a woman who yearned to understand the large movements in life but was better than I was at accepting mysteries no one would ever solve.

Afterward we drove to the beach and walked in the sand. At home that night I felt a thickness in the air, but the presence had changed, beginning to leave us like a season or a storm. Lying next to Jolene, I ran my fingers through her hair, but she didn't dream. Her fingers didn't move, her knees didn't twitch, she didn't open her mouth in an attempt to impart secrets of another world. She simply lay there, at times turning or gathering the blankets around her body. Late at night, around three o'clock, I was drawn under as well.

The dreams didn't come the next night, nor the night after that. And after a month, we both knew that they'd left us, offering only the outline of an idea without color or texture. For weeks I'd find her examining art slides, hoping to well up that desperate curiosity again, but eventually she returned to her old afternoon activities, reading textbooks or reviewing her lecture notes. The following month, I went back to writing. I tried to change the ending of my first essay, but found that I could not. After a while I understood that it was the true ending for that essay—or at least *one* true ending—because a story is tied to experience and experience is tied to an individual and to a particular time. For months that ending was true for me, and even now, three years later, I can see its truth, but I understand it belongs to a person I was some years ago. I understand, too, that Sam Browne exists in the past, that I cannot go back and be him or even understand him exactly as he understood himself. He exists in my essays and in memory, but I hold on to him differently now, as we all must hold on to those people we were some time ago. He is a kind of friend, and I draw a strength from that connection, but each day I sense how that connection changes a little. He returned to me long enough so I could write about him. That, I think, is all one can ask from memory.

In the weeks between summer school and the regular semester, Jolene and I spent a lot of time together, long August days in the townhouse or down by the water, where seagulls speckled the horizon. We talked about many things, including our dreams about the valley, but could never come to any conclusions about what it all meant: we could read the experiences only as the dreams they were and could not place them into a larger context even though elements in the dreams compelled us to do so. Together, we looked at my sketches of the valley, their perspectives oddly buoyant, and then we read through my grandmother's journals one last time before I put them back in their box and stored them in the den.

By Christmas, I'd written five essays about Australia, but saw how each of them was lacking in certain ways because they were unable to pull together my family's entire story. I started revising them, and as I did, I understood that the presence which had entered our house the previous summer had left us for good, imparting no specific knowledge, just a series of images and odd declarative statements, a small whirlwind twisting in that other realm we could not truly understand. I thought Jolene and I might change back into the people we'd been the previous year, but that didn't happen either. We'd been shadowed by this experience, baptized and changed, and each evening when I saw her reading in bed or correcting another set of quizzes, I saw a longing in her eyes directed at me. I knew, as well, this longing was in me and was directed at her. I'd never felt such a sustained hopefulness before, a feeling I imagine must have been like the ones that filled my mother and grandmother: it was expansive, but in our case not dangerous.

The following March I decided to return my grandmother's manuscripts to Australia, to the Museum of Australian History, one of the four museums that had requested ownership of them. As Jolene and I were boxing them up in special metal shipping containers, I thought I'd learned everything about my grandmother I was able to know, that I'd drawn careful lines to connect the points of her life. But I knew there were considerable gaps, things that no one could ever know, an odd sense of distance that sometimes made me feel as if I didn't really know her despite all I had read. We dropped off the containers at the airport, and the following day heard that they'd arrived in Sydney and would be featured in an exhibit called "Pioneering Women of Eastern Australia." My grandmother's journals would be included in a section called "The Modern Movement" that showed how women had helped break down the Imperialist sentiments of the previous century.

For a while, I thought my story would end here, with the shipping of my grandmother's manuscripts back to the country I believed truly owned them, but the story did not end. It continued for many months.

My grandmother remained a strong presence in my life. I found I thought of her quite often, and I knew that Jolene thought of her as well. It was a gift, I realized, this strange connection to my grandmother: it was one of the things that stitched me and Jolene together.

That August we were married at City Hall, and the following summer, when we took a belated honeymoon to Australia, I was very conscious of how the country had changed. It was no longer my grandmother's country, nor was it the Australia I'd known when I'd lived there with my mother. Throughout Sydney, the language had softened, the accents smoothed out, eroded by foreign TV and international movies. The city itself was littered with McDonald's and Pizza Huts. Along the train tracks, I saw graffiti scrawled like strange advertisements I couldn't decipher. My grandmother's story was still well-known in many areas: I found her book in five small stores. In the large downtown Dymock's there were nine copies featured in a display of regional authors. The stage play about her life had finished its run; the tapes of radio drama were out of print, but I still felt something of my grandmother here and believed her legacy continued to change the country in small ways, by asking people to reconsider what it meant to be a woman and to be Australian.

At a pub in the Blue Mountains, Jolene asked the bartender, "Where did *that woman* go into the valley?" Of course Jolene knew the exact place, had read about it in my stories, but wanted to see if other people still remembered. Just by the phrase *that woman*, the bartender knew to whom she referred. "The woman who went a-walking," he said. "Yes, she went down by them there Sisters. There used to be a sign, but someone pinched it a few years back." For the rest of the day, we walked around the mountains, past my grandmother's old cottage, its exterior no longer green and gold, but repainted sandstone with a brown trim. From the street, we looked in her old windows, but saw no one, only half-empty bookshelves and a chandelier. Most of my uncle's plants had been replaced with plants I didn't recognize, and on their roof, attached to the chimney, the new owners had anchored a small satellite dish.

Later that afternoon, we went to the visitors' center, where we saw many displays on Aboriginal life and on ecological conservation in the valley. We walked down the Giant Stairway, making the trip I had not made in my essay, the very steps my mother and grandmother used to follow, the same steps I'd walked with my first girlfriend, Kelly. At the bottom, the valley opened up, the branches becoming canopies, a dirt trail curving along cliffs, the same path I remembered from my boyhood, though it was much wider now, more developed. We walked past sandstone boulders and waterfalls. For a while we held a piece of my family's history, its presence still pure and warm, mingled with air and mist and the sunlight that webbed its way through gum trees and stippled the ground around us.

When we left the greater Sydney area, I assumed we wouldn't hear about my grandmother again. We made our way around the country, touching down in Melbourne, Alice Springs, and finally Perth, on the opposite coast, where the vast Indian Ocean rolled over the shore. We'd intended to stay three nights, but after two Jolene suggested we leave early and drive north. She'd seen photos of two northern towns and wanted to explore them. In a small town called Quincy, we checked in at a pub and hotel called the Woman of

Stone. After drinking a few schooners of beer, we asked two men who appeared to be locals about the name. "Oh that," one of them said, "it was a bit of a curio a few years back, brought a fair few tourists in."

"It did," the other confirmed.

"This white woman, she came walking out of the bush, no shoes, no hat, barely a stitch on her. She was all done up like the Abos. I mean with face paint. Mumbling that she was stone. From what I heard, that's all she said."

"She was fifty-five, maybe sixty years old," the other said. "Old, you understand, but not too old. They thought she had a touch of heatstroke, would pull through and come good, but sometime that night she died. When the nurse came to check on her, she looked like a woman of eighty-five or ninety, like all the life had been taken from her in that one night. And this is the other weird bit, they find this piece of paper in her hand, something she'd scribbled about Australia."

"If you ask me," the first man said, "it's a good yarn, but it's been exaggerated."

"How long ago did all this happen?" I asked.

"Kind of hard to say," he said. "Seven, might be eight

years ago."

"Somewhere around there, I reckon," the other said.

We drank our beers while the two of them talked about other things, rugby and a new highway being paved, whether or not we remembered the year the Australians had won the America's Cup, which we did. The entire time, though, I was thinking about the story they'd told us, as I knew Jolene was, and when we finished our drinks, we left them and walked to the hotel lobby where, framed on the wall, we found old newspaper clippings about the Woman of Stone who had, almost seven years to the date, wandered into town, her feet bare, her hair matted with a fragrant oil.

The photos of course showed my grandmother, or at least a woman who looked a great deal like her. In the first, a black-and-white shot, her face was very tan, two lines of white paint crossed each cheek, her chin was dotted black. She appeared to be about sixty, her eyes still holding those old questions. In the second, she was at the hospital, her face clean, her expression confused, but in the third and final photo, she'd been transformed into a woman at least thirty years older, wrinkles deep across her face, eyes closed, her skin loose, lips pale as paper, and in her hand, written on the back of a hospital form, was her last message, the idea she must've clung to shortly before she died: "And Australia will be its own nation, will rise and become great again." There was no photo of the note by itself, but from the way the words were put together, their exact rhythm, I had a good idea how the individual letters would've been formed, the slant of the writing, the sloped Ts, and I thought it appropriate that my grandmother—if it was in fact her—would've left such a note. It was the idea she most hoped would become true.

In the most recent clipping, dated a year later than the others, a local journalist explained that after months of searching in Perth and its surrounding communities the authorities had no better idea who the woman might've been than when she arrived, nor did doctors have any better explanation for her dramatic aging, though one regional physician thought it might have been the result of a rare retrovirus.

We did not stay the night in Quincy as we had planned, but instead put our luggage back into our rented car and started out on the highway. We drove quietly for a while, holding this secret between us, the only people who knew the two halves of my grandmother's story, its thickness worked around us like the presence of that dream. When we returned to Sydney, I'd tell my uncle, but I wasn't sure if I'd tell anyone else. At least not for a while. Above us, stars speckled the sky and, for the first time in over a year, I thought about them as my grandmother had, like little pinholes shining through to heaven. I thought, too, about time the way she had, if it could be compacted like an accordion, rearranged by our will. I wondered if, by choice, we lived in a scientific world, ignoring other important aspects of our existence, like those coded into stories. I liked to believe that science could be trumped by stories, that there was part of us science could never explain, but I didn't know if that was true or not. By the time we were passing through the next small town, I realized Jolene was looking at me and had been for a while.

"Sometimes," she said, "I feel very strange here. In Australia, I mean, like I was meant to come here. At least for a little while."

"I always feel like that when I'm in Australia," I said. "No matter how many times I come here I can never shake the feeling, that I'm here for a reason."

"You're a romantic," she said, smiling, "and I imagine that someday I'll regret that I married a romantic."

"I doubt you'll regret it," I said, and then looking at her, I saw a small stream of air feathering through her hair. "Are you still scared about loving me?"

"At times," she said.

"What scares you?"

She glanced at the distant stars, before turning back to me, a hopefulness in her eyes. "Because," she said, "I have no idea how to hold on to you. That's the hardest part."

I was about to tell her the same thing, that I had no idea how to hold on to her, but realized this might be the thing that would actually save us, this wanting, this risk, this sense of hope. Instead, I placed my hand over hers. Outside the road was lined with gum trees and wattle, their silhouettes sprouting from the ground, thick and dark against the sky. Every hour or so, we passed another waystation, and by two in the morning, I knew we'd travel all night, that we were buckled in for the long haul, hoping that when the sun came up, light slanting down through a thin layer of clouds, we'd find

that we'd arrived someplace good, still in my grandmother's country but in a place that at least for a day
we might also call our own.

ACKNOWLEDGMENTS

My gratitude goes out to the following people and institutions: To William, my constant friend in Sydney. To my mother and sister. To Adam, who helped me understand what it means to have vision. To Jarret, who put up with my neuroses. To Ryan, Miles, Chris, Mark, and Virgil who made graduate school worthwhile. Of course to Jerry and Kevin. To Anika, for her amazing edits and perfect advice. To Dorothy, for her book design. To MacAdam/Cage, especially Melanie and Tasha, and David and Scott, for believing in this novel. To *American Literary Review*, *The Literary Review*, *The Missouri Review*, and *The Seattle Review*, where portions of this novel first appeared. To the following universities for their support: Oregon State University, University of California at Irvine, Florida State University. And of course to Kerry, without whom I would be lost.